TWO WOMEN TRIED TO WARN HIM.
HE LISTENED TO ONE. . . .

She lifted her wrist provocatively, and my Spanish gold piece on her bracelet flashed in front of me.

It was Manny Mannix's girl. "Manny told me you've got something he wants," she said.

"That's the way Manny lives—wanting something someone else has."

"This time he swears he's going to get it."

"He'll have to find me first, and he'll be a long time looking. And even if he does find me . . ."

I was moving away as I spoke, but she stopped me in my tracks.

"When he finds you, Commander . . . when he finds you, he's going to kill you!"

GALLOWS ON THE SAND

GALLOWS
on the
SAND

Morris West

BANTAM BOOKS
TORONTO · NEW YORK · LONDON · SYDNEY · AUCKLAND

This low-priced Bantam Book
has been completely reset in a type face
designed for easy reading, and was printed
from new plates. It contains the complete
text of the original hard-cover edition.
NOT ONE WORD HAS BEEN OMITTED.

GALLOWS ON THE SAND

A Bantam Book / published by arrangement with
William Morrow & Co., Inc.

PRINTING HISTORY

This title was previously published as a part of A WEST QUARTET
by William Morrow, September 1981

Bantam edition / June 1984

ISBN 0-553-24248-3

Published simultaneously in the United States and Canada

Bantam Books are published by Bantam Books, Inc. Its trademark, consisting of
the words "Bantam Books" and the portrayal of a rooster, is Registered in U.S.
Patent and Trademark Office and in other countries. Marca Registrada. Bantam
Books, Inc., 666 Fifth Avenue, New York, New York 10103.

PRINTED IN THE UNITED STATES OF AMERICA

H   0 9 8 7 6 5 4 3 2 1

GALLOWS
on the
SAND

Chapter One

The letter was delivered to my room at a quarter past twelve on Wednesday, the thirtieth of June. It was addressed to Mr. Renn Lundigan, Department of History, University of Sydney, Sydney, Australia.

There was a baroque seal on the flap of the envelope and an address in Spanish in the lower left-hand corner. The postmark was slightly askew and the typescript was fine and clear.

I remember all these things so clearly because I looked at the envelope for a long, long time before I dared to open it.

Finally I picked up a paper knife, slit the envelope carefully, took out the folded sheet and sat down, lit a cigarette and began to read.

The man who had written the letter was the Chief Archivist of the City of Acapulco, Mexico.

He told me with Latin flourish of the interest my inquiry had awakened in his department. He told me of his eagerness to establish so definite a link between the Spanish navigators of the eighteenth century and the new continent, Terra Australis Incognita. He told me how gratified he was to cooperate with so scholarly a gentleman on so important a piece of historical research.

He told me that in October 1732 the *Doña Lucia* had left Acapulco with twenty chests of minted gold for the colonies of His Most Catholic Majesty in the Philippine Islands.

That the *Doña Lucia* had never arrived at Manila and was presumed either to have foundered in a storm or fallen victim to pirates in the China seas.

That the gold coin of which I had sent such an excellent rubbing was of a minting contemporary with the *Doña Lucia* and could in fact have been part of her cargo.

He told me . . .

But the rest was courtesy and I was no longer interested.

I was thinking of a tiny island off the coast of Queensland, one of the hundred islands and atolls strung like chips of jade and emerald along the coral thread of the Great Barrier Reef.

A two-horned island, sheer to the sea on one side, with a narrow crescent of white beach on the other. An island where the winter tourists never came, because the surveys of the Queensland Government said there was no water there, and no channel through the reefs and no shelter for fishing boats or cabin cruisers.

But I knew there was a channel. Jeannette and I had run a thirty-footer clean through the reef and beached her without a scratch on her copper sheathing. We had camped for days under the pandanus and found a spring at the foot of the western horn. We had walked the reef and gone spearfishing at high tide, and one day Jeannette had brought up a gold chain, defaced, encrusted with coral.

Then, before our honeymoon was past a month, Jeannette had died of meningitis and I was left—with a junior lectureship, a battered coin and the dream of a golden girl on a white beach in the sun. And the dream of a Spanish treasure ship under rioting coral branches.

The memory of Jeannette faded slowly, faded to a dull ache in my heart that flared occasionally into savage pain and drove me to wild nights of drinking and chasing my luck with the baccarat boys and the hardheads round the poker table, and the strappers who stood round the tracks in the misty morning trying to pick Saturday's winners.

The memory of Jeannette faded, but whenever I opened the drawer of my desk the old coin, burnished from daily handling, seemed to glow like fire. My girl was gone, lost to me for life, but my treasure ship was there. It must be there—timbers rotted, decks canted under the coral and the sea grasses, while the rainbow fish swam round and round the treasure chests in the hold.

It must be there. I was a historian. I could prove it must be there. At least I must prove it *could* be there.

It was old Anson who gave me the clue—George Baron Anson, not yet an Admiral of the Fleet, not yet First Lord of the Admiralty, cruising months on end between the Ladrones and the Carolines, waiting for the galleons that came every year from Acapulco to Manila. George Anson, who literally lashed his leaky hulk together so that he could wait another month and another while the barnacles grew on his hulk and his water casks split and his men died of scurvy under the tropic sun.

The old Spaniard would come nosing out of Acapulco, sniffing for the northeast trades that would drive him westward along the equatorial belt until it was time to tack north again past the Ladrones to Manila . . . but October would be late for him. Summer would be drifting down towards Capricorn, and if he drove too far south the hurricanes might catch him. And if the hurricanes caught him—they would whirl him down, past the Bismarcks and the Solomons, and westward on to the Great Barrier. He would be under jury rig by now, listing perhaps and leaking, in no condition to thread his way through the islands and the reefs. And if the weather did not blow itself out, one day, one night, perhaps, the coral claws would rake him open and he would founder—on the outer reef of an island with twin horns.

It could have happened like that, it must have happened like that. Else where did my doubloon come from, that dull golden eye that mocked me from the bottom of my drawer?

There was a knock at my door and the little blonde from the registrar's office came in with a wire tray stacked with pay envelopes.

She smiled and fluttered her eyelashes and shifted the tray so that I could see what her sweater did for her figure, and made her little joke when she handed me the envelope.

"Don't spend it all at once, Mr. Lundigan."

I smiled and said thank you and then made my little joke.

"Let me take you out one night and I'll spend some of it on you."

She giggled as she always did, lifted her chest a little higher, picked up her tray and walked out, swinging her hips.

I tore the top from the envelope and tipped its contents on my blotter. Two fivers, eight singles and some assorted silver, the weekly stipend—less tax—of a junior lecturer in history.

Take a week's board out of that and cigarette money and tram fares and the pound I'd borrowed from Jenkins on Tuesday, that left enough for a stake at Manny's. But not enough, not nearly enough to buy an island and a boat and diving gear and stores and help and all the other things a man needs when he starts looking for sunken treasure, and then trying to raise it when he has found it.

Still, it was a stake. And last week I had seen a fellow turn a fiver into five hundred and then into a thousand

and then into two thousand. After which Manny sent him home in a hired car, with one of his own bruisers for safe conduct. I had seen it done. Perhaps I could do it myself.

I wouldn't even need two thousand. One would be enough. Five hundred for the island. The Queensland Government sells cheap when there is no water and no channel and no harbourage. Two hundred for a boat—no cabin cruiser at that. A hundred for new diving gear. That would leave two hundred for incidentals and there'd be more than enough of those, but it could be done . . . if I won a thousand pounds at Manny's.

I folded the letter from the Chief Archivist of Acapulco and put it in my pocket. I took the gold piece from the drawer and slipped it into my fob, for luck. I counted out eight pounds, ten shillings, and sealed them in an envelope. At least I would eat and sleep with a roof over my head and take a tram to work and smoke twenty cigarettes a day . . . if I didn't win a thousand pounds at Manny's.

The junior lectureship in history does not carry a private telephone, so I had to walk down the hall and fumble in my pocket for pennies before I could make my call.

A laconic voice said, "This is Charlie."

"This is the Commander. Where is it?"

"Same as last week. It's a clear night."

"Thanks."

I hung up. It was a clear night. The police had been paid and Manny would not be raided tonight. I would have my chance to win a thousand pounds.

You should meet Manny Mannix.

He's quite a boy. Brooklyn Irish on his father's side, Brooklyn Italian on his mother's. Manny was a supply sergeant with the United States Army who fought a gallant war from King's Cross and, when the war was over, decided to stay in Sydney.

Sydney, according to Manny, was New York cut down to workable size, and Manny was ready and willing to work it. He worked the disposals racket and the sly-grog racket and the used-car racket and the immigration racket, and when the profits started to slide, Manny slid out, too, with a bank balance that bought him a block of flats, a slice of a nightclub and a string of assorted fillies whom he paraded for the decorative effect. Manny was never a man to let love interfere with business. Manny also bought himself a small piece of the gaming squad—enough to guarantee him a phone call before the cars turned into his street.

For Manny that was more than enough . . . life was too sweet to spoil it with a conviction. Manny dressed well and ate well and drove a Cadillac as long as a housefront, but no matter what he wore or where he dined, he carried always the stink of the city, the smell of stale women and the reek of racket money.

You should meet Manny Mannix.

He calls me Commander because in an unguarded moment I told him I ran a lugger round the Trobriands in the last years of the war. He pumps my hand and slaps my shoulder and offers me a drink which I never refuse. While we drink, Manny talks. About Manny, about money and Manny, about girls and Manny and Manny's plans for Manny's future. And while he talks he smiles, but never with his eyes, which dart from the bouncers at the door to the tense little groups round the tables and the stewards moving about with trays of drinks held shoulder-high.

You should meet Manny.

You would hate him as much as I do; but you might not hate yourself as much as I do, because I drink his liquor and listen to his patter and smile at his jokes, because I want to preserve the privilege of losing my money at his game and having Manny pat me tolerantly on the shoulder and tell me better luck next time.

If I won tonight, there would be no next time. I would cash my chips and go, and turn my face to a green island and a white beach and a golden hoard where the reef dropped down into deep water.

So, at nine o'clock on Wednesday night, the thirtieth of June, I hailed a taxi and drove out past the flying-boat base at Rose Bay to a discreet crescent near Vaucluse. On the loop of the crescent there was a high stone wall, broken by gates of wrought iron.

The gates were locked, but there was a bell push on the pillar, and when I pressed it a man came out from the lodgekeeper's cottage. I told him it was a clear night. He made no argument about it but opened the small side gate and let me in.

I walked up the gravelled drive to the house. The curtains were drawn and the shutters were closed, but the front door was open and I saw men and women who might have been guests at a cocktail party and a waiter in a white coat crossing the carpeted hall.

I nodded to the sad-eyed Pole who kept the door, handed him my overcoat and went upstairs to the big room with the black-glass bar and the great windows that would show you the lights of the harbour, if they were opened—but they never were.

To run a business like Manny's, you need to shut out the moon and the stars and the wind that comes in from wide waters. You must draw the drapes and close out the cheep of crickets and the silken wash of the ebb tide. You must have music and laughter and the click of the wheel and the clack of the counters stacked and unstacked on the baize. You must have strong liquor and stale smoke and the shabby illusion of friendship and community.

To run a business like Manny's, you wear shining pumps and knife-creased black trousers and a silver-grey tuxedo with a burgundy tie and a red carnation in your buttonhole. You take your elbow off the bar when your

guest comes in, you toss a wink to the model draped on
the corner stool, and you say:

"Hiya, Commander! Long time no see."

"Hiya, Manny! Long time no money."

I delivered my line with a little smile and Manny
laughed and choked on his cigar smoke. He took me by
the elbow and steered me to the stool next to the model.
He tapped the bar and called to the steward.

"Set one up for the Commander, Frank. Pink gin.
Commander, I'd like you to meet a friend of mine, Miss
June Dolan. June, this is Commander Lundigan. Watch
out for him, sweetheart. You know what these navy boys
are."

Manny choked again and grinned, and the model gave
me a small professional smile and a long professional look
that set my six-foot figure against Manny's six-figure
prospects and found me wanting. Which was exactly
what Manny knew she would do. Otherwise he would
never have introduced me.

Manny said, "You feeling lucky tonight, Commander?"

I shrugged and spread my hands and made a rueful
mouth. It's a little act. I do it very well. Jeannette used to
tell me it was part of my boyish charm. Now I felt rather
ashamed of it. It was so like the smile of Manny's
drooping model.

"Not more than usual, Manny. But I could use it, if it
runs."

"I guess we all could at that," said Manny. "Say,
Commander, what do you think of this?"

He closed his hand round the model's limp fingers and
lifted her forearm to display a heavy gold bracelet hung
with coins.

"I bought it for her today. It's the little sweetheart's
birthday and I thought, that's for my baby. So I waltzed
right in and bought it. Cost a packet, too. But I reckon
she's worth it. What do you think of it, Commander?"

"I think it fits the lady's personality."

"See, there's room for more coins on it. So I say to her, if she's a good girl and brings me luck, I'll fill it up for her, link by link."

"I'm dry, Manny," said the model. Her voice was flat and bored.

Manny frowned and tapped the counter and the steward sidled up to refill the lady's glass. The coins jingled dully as she took her hand away from Manny and began to fumble in her handbag. It was then I had my foolish idea.

I took the gold piece out of my pocket, spun it in the air and laid it on the bar.

"Talking of coins, Manny—have you ever seen one of those before?"

A flicker of interest showed in Manny's guarded eyes. He took the coin, examined it and made a tiny nick in the edge with his diamond ring.

"It's gold?"

"Pure gold. I keep it for a good-luck piece."

I popped the coin back in my pocket and watched with some satisfaction the gleam in Manny's eyes.

"What sort of coin is it, Commander?"

"Spanish. Eighteenth century. There's a story about it."

"I'd like to hear it sometime."

This was the lead I had hoped for. Manny smelt gold. Manny might be prepared to lay out paper to catch gold. I said, as casually as I could, "As a matter of fact, Manny, there's a proposition behind that gold piece. One that might interest you."

Manny's eyes were instantly hooded. His voice took on the flat, incurious tone of the huckster.

"Well, you know me, Commander. Always interested in any proposition, provided it's profitable—and safe. Like to talk about it now?"

I shook my head.

"Later, Manny."

Later I might have a thousand pounds and then I wouldn't have to discuss my proposition with Manny. I wouldn't have to say a single word to Manny—ever again.

"Later it is, Commander," Manny said, and turned back to the bar and the drooping model with the round bosom, the flat voice and the shrewd professional eyes.

One hour and seven minutes later I was back at the bar—flat broke and busted.

Chapter Two

"Drink, Commander?" said Manny.

I refused, wearily.

"Sorry, Manny, can't afford it. I'm cleaned out."

Manny clicked his tongue and made little soothing gestures.

"Too bad, Commander—too bad. It comes and it goes. I figure the house owes the loser a drink. Sit down."

"No thanks, Manny. It's a nice thought, but I'll be running along."

I moved towards the door, but Manny followed me. I had never known him so reluctant to speed the losing guest.

"Commander?"

"Yes, Manny?"

"You said something about a proposition. Like to talk about it in my office?"

So I had hooked him after all. My heart was thumping and my mouth was dry. I had to clench my fists to stop the trembling of my fingers, but I tried to make my answer sound indifferent.

"Just as you like. There's no hurry."

"This way, Commander," Manny said, and steered me through a leather-studded door onto an acre of mushroom carpet under a chandelier of Murano glass.

There were mushroom draperies with gold cords.

There was a buhl desk with a high-backed chair in Italian walnut. There was a fabulous settee in gold brocade in front of an Adam fireplace, and the drinks were served from a cabinet concealed in the pastel panelling. The fairies from the Cross had done Manny proud. Everything was genuine, everything was expensive, and the final effect was as true to character as the foyer in the House of All Nations . . . and as depressing.

Manny gave me a sidelong look as he bent over the drinks.

"You like it, Commander?"

I clicked my tongue and said, "It must have cost you plenty, Manny."

Which Manny took for a compliment and grinned and said, "It even frightens *me*, how much. Still, I work here, so I figure I might as well be comfortable. Besides, it impresses the clients."

"I didn't think the clients ever got in here, Manny."

I winked and smiled at him over the glass, the brothers-in-lechery smile, which makes a man like Manny push out his chest and forget that he has to buy what other men have for love.

Manny winked back and raised his glass.

"To the fillies . . . God bless 'em."

We drank. Then Manny waved me to the settee, while he himself stood back against the Adam fireplace, his elbows resting on the marble mantel. I recognized the gambit. It's hard to sit down and sell anything to a man who is standing up. You should try it sometime. I decided to make myself as comfortable as possible. I leant back against the gold brocade, crossed my knees and tried to feel relaxed, while I waited for Manny to open the discussion.

Manny's eyes were hooded again, filmed over like a bird's, so that there was no light or luster in them. When he spoke his voice was soft, almost caressing.

"What line of business are you in, Commander?"

"Does it matter?"

Manny pinched the end from an expensive cigar and took his time over lighting it. When it was drawing well, he blew a cloud of smoke and waved the cigar in the direction of the door.

"Out there at the tables—no, it doesn't matter. A man pays for his drinks. If he loses he pays for his chips. If he wins he doesn't make a fuss. That's all I want to know. You're a man like that, Commander. I like to have you here. But this is different. This is business. In business you've got to work together. So I've got to know."

He put the cigar back in his mouth, drew on it and waited.

I grinned at him—a nice friendly grin, no malice in it at all. I said, "Just for curiosity, Manny, what do you think is my business?"

Manny blew out more smoke and pursed his lips and said, "I've often tried to figure that, Commander. You're not Service, although you've got the Service look. Guess a navy guy never really loses that. You could be wool money, but you don't spend big enough. You play cautious, and when you're out of chips you quit. You could be an agent, though you don't have the salesman look. Doctor, dentist, maybe. Like I told you, I've never been able to figure for sure."

"I'm a historian."

His cigar almost fell out of his mouth.

"A what?"

"A historian. I lecture in history at the University of Sydney."

Manny was puzzled. It showed behind the film that covered his eyes. I had made ground. If I could hold it I might have a chance. Manny gave himself time to recover before he shot his next question at me.

"How much does that pay?"

"Eleven hundred a year . . . twelve with extension lectures."

"Peanuts," said Manny concisely. "For a guy with brains—peanuts."

"That's why I'm interested in business."

Manny shook his head. "For business, you need capital. What have you got?"

I stood up and spun the coin under his nose again. "I've got this."

"How much is it worth?"

"For the gold—about six pounds, Australian. As an antique, about thirty. I've had it valued."

"With that, maybe, you could start in the popcorn business, Commander, but that's not for Manny Mannix."

This was the critical moment. If I said the wrong thing now I was lost and my treasure ship was lost, too. I said nothing. I smiled. I took my glass over to the cabinet and made myself another drink. This made Manny puzzled again, puzzled and interested. I brought my drink back to the fire and toasted him. Then I said, "The trouble with fellows like you, Manny, you think you know all the answers. Nobody can tell you."

Manny flushed but he kept his temper.

"So you should tell me anything, Commander. I got all I want . . . and it's all paid for with dough to spare in the bank. What should you tell me that I don't know?"

"Where this coin came from, for instance."

"Well, spill it. Where did it come from?"

"From a Spanish galleon that left Acapulco for Manila in October 1732 and was lost with all hands."

Manny relaxed and grinned skeptically.

"Treasure stories, huh? Oldest sucker bait known. You got a map, too? Old pirate map maybe? Pick 'em up for five dollars apiece anywhere round the Caribbean. Like shrunken heads, the locals make 'em for the tourist trade."

I shook my head.

"No map."

"Well, go on, what have you got?"

I took the letter out of my pocket and showed it to him. He read it painfully, fumbling for the facts behind the courtly phrases and the stilted English. Then he looked at me and tapped the letter with his thumb.

"This genuine?"

"It is. Nobody forges a document like that. Only costs a cable to prove it true or false."

Manny nodded. So much he could understand.

"Yeah . . . yeah. Guess that's right. But it doesn't say enough. There was a treasure ship. This coin could have come from it. Doesn't say it did come from it."

"That's where I come in. I'm a historian, as I told you. It's my job to collect, weigh and determine the value of historical evidence. I've collected enough evidence to show that the lost galleon could have been wrecked near the spot where I found that coin."

"Where was that?"

I was sure of him now. He wasn't waving his cigar anymore. The film had slipped from his eyes and I read greed and interest and the calculations of the trader weighing cost against revenue to determine the percentage profit. I could play him more firmly now, like a tiring fish at the end of his run. I told him bluntly.

"The place is my secret. I know where it is. I found this coin there myself. I'm not prepared to reveal it until we've made and signed a legal agreement."

"How much do you want?"

"For a half share—a thousand pounds, and all expenses paid."

So it was done. The chips were down. There was no more to do or say. The next play was up to Manny Mannix.

But Manny wasn't ready to bid yet. He had more questions to ask.

"Suppose we did find this ship—where you say it

should be—how much of this stuff could we expect to get?"

"The letter says twenty chests of gold. I couldn't guess what it might be worth . . . twenty thousand, thirty . . . something like that. Could be a lot more, of course."

"Could be. Could also be that this place was salted and then we'd get nothing."

"Could be," I agreed. "But it wasn't. I know that. My wife and I brought up the coin."

Manny shot me a quick inquiring glance. "You didn't tell me you were married."

"My wife died a month after the wedding day."

Manny clucked and said, "Too bad," then handed me the next inquiry. "You said you wanted a thousand for yourself and all expenses paid. What sort of expenses did you have in mind, Commander?"

"Two thousand pounds—more or less. You might do it on less, but you'd be working the hard way."

"What sort of items would that include?"

Manny was so obviously interested, we had so obviously progressed from speculative bargaining to practical thinking, that I forgot to be cautious.

I gave him the answer, clear and simple.

"Five hundred to buy the island. That would give you land and water rights and a way round the law of treasure trove. Then there's a cabin cruiser and diving gear equipment and stores and perhaps a professional diver for the later stages. I could give you an itemized list when we get round to it."

I had dug my own pit and walked myself happily into it, but I didn't know it then. I didn't know it till much later. At that moment I didn't even know why Manny was smiling. When he turned away to mix our third drink, I thought he was preparing to seal our bargain. Which proved I didn't know Manny. Which proved I was what Manny thought I was: a simpleminded historian, who couldn't read the elementary lessons of history, which are the vanity of human wishes and the fickleness of women and the fact that no sucker ever gets an even break—because he doesn't deserve it.

Manny came back with the drinks. We raised our glasses and smiled at each other across the rims. Then Manny said, quite gently, "Sorry, Commander . . . no dice."

It was as final as a smack in the mouth.

And Manny smiled and smiled and smiled.

I wasn't smiling. I felt sick and tired and humiliated, and I wanted to go home. Then Manny moved in for his final punch.

"Tell you what, Commander. Just to show there's no ill feeling, I'll buy the coin for the market price—thirty quid. Look nice on the little girl's bracelet."

I laughed myself then. God knows why, but I laughed. I spun the coin and caught it and said to Manny, "Give me a free night at the bar as well and it's a deal."

Manny looked at me with cold contempt, then went over to the buhl desk and counted out thirty pounds in crisp new notes. He snapped a rubber band round them and laid them flat in my outstretched hand. He said, "If you're wise, Commander, you'll leave the tables alone and stick to the bar. The drinks are on the house like you wanted."

"Thanks, Manny," I said. "Thanks and good night."

"Good night," said Manny. "Good night, sucker."

I remember walking to the bar and ordering a double Scotch.

After that, nothing.

At nine o'clock the next morning the dean found me snoring in the shrubbery outside his front window.

At four o'clock the same afternoon the faculty accepted my resignation and gave me a month's pay in lieu of notice. Which left me with a screaming hangover, no job, no prospects and a little better than a hundred pounds in cash. For Manny had been kind to me. When he had bundled me out into the street, he had pinned his thirty pounds into my inside pocket with a note:

"Too bad, Commander. It was a nice play."

Manny is like that. A friendly fellow, with a sense of humour.

Chapter Three

On Friday morning I went out to collect a debt.

I took the early train to Camden, which is a small, smug little town built on the wealth of the oldest landed gentry of the youngest country in the world. The green pastures sweep up to its doorsteps and the black bitumen highway winds through acres on rolling acres of fat grazing land, dappled with shade from the great white gums and the willows that fringe the homestead creeks. The mellow grey houses are set far back in the folds of the land and the families who own them go back to the First Fleet and the raw, roistering days of a convict colony.

This is stud country, all of it; dairy country, merino country, sleek, horsebreeders' country where a drought never comes and the creeks are never dry and the roots go deep and where I, a rootless man from the city, had no place.

In Camden I hired a taxi and drove out five miles along the highway to a chain-wire gate, over which was raised, pergola fashion, the legend—McAndrew Stud. It's a longish walk from the gate to the homestead, and the taxi man stared at me when I paid him off and told him to call back for me in an hour's time.

He couldn't know that I was ashamed of my errand and of myself and that I needed the walk between the flowering gums to prepare for my meeting with Alistair McAndrew.

The drive rose gently for a while and then dipped down to the house, a low spreading sandstone building nestling in shrubbery and ringed by white outbuildings and the fences of the home paddocks.

To the left was a broad pasture with some of the McAndrew stock at grass. To the right was a small enclosure of tanbark, where a group of men were watching a young colt being broken to the saddle.

McAndrew was with them—a stocky black Celt in khaki shirt and riding breeches. He leant on the rail fence in the relaxed attitude of the country man, but his puckered eyes missed no detail of the exercise and from time to time he called a quiet direction to the strapper in the saddle.

He turned at my footfall, hesitated a moment, then came towards me with a wide smile and hand outstretched.

"Lundigan! Well, I'll be damned! Man, it's good to see you!"

I grinned foolishly and pumped his hand and said, banally enough, "Hullo, Mac."

"What brings you out Camden way?"

"Well, I . . . . I wanted to see you, Mac. If you've got time, that is."

My voice, or my eyes, betrayed me then, because he looked at me with odd concern and said, "Of course, man. All the time in the world. Excuse me a minute while I have a word with the boys."

I watched him as he turned away to give directions to the men around the training enclosure. He walked with assurance, talked with authority, a man at home and at ease with his men and his horses and his dappled acres. I remembered the day when I had dragged him across a beach in the Trobriands, a yellow, shrunken skeleton, last survivor of a raiding party whom the Japanese had cut to pieces two days after they landed. Shaking with malaria, knotted by dysentery, he had made his way to the rendezvous, and we had brought him off under fire from the patrol in the palm groves . . .and now I had come to claim payment.

McAndrew came back and we walked together towards the house.

"It's been a long time, Renn."

"Eleven years . . . twelve. Yes . . . a long time, Mac."

"My wife's in town for the day. She'd like to meet you. You'll stay, of course. I've a lot to show you."

I shook my head. "I'm sorry, Mac. I have to leave in an hour."

He was puzzled and a little hurt. He pressed the point.

"But you can't blow in and blow out like this. Of course you must stay."

"Perhaps you'd better hear why I've come, first."

It was a graceless, mumbling sort of answer to give to a man you haven't seen in twelve years; and yet, what else was there to say? I felt awkward, loutish. I was sorry I had come.

He took my elbow and steered me gently across the veranda and into the living room, a wide expanse of polished floor with bright rugs and good pictures and leather chairs grouped about a great stone fireplace.

"Make yourself easy, Renn. I'll fix a drink. Scotch?"

"Thanks."

The armchair was deep and comfortable, but I could not relax. The muscles of my face were tight, my mouth was dry. My hands were unsteady and I pressed them hard against the arms of the chair to stop their trembling. McAndrew brought the drinks, handed me mine and then sat down, facing me across the fireplace.

"Good health, Renn—and happy meetings!"

"Good health, Mac."

The whisky went down, smoothly, as a good whisky should, and then lay like a warm coal at the pit of my stomach. McAndrew watched me with sober concern.

"Renn, are you ill?"

"Ill?" I tried to laugh, but it was a dry, coughing sound in my throat. "No, not ill. At least not the way a doctor would read it."

"A friend might read it differently."

His gentleness, his puzzlement, his genuine kindness, made me suddenly angry with myself. I heaved myself out of my chair and stood by the fireplace looking down at him. The words seemed to force themselves out, rasping my throat as they came.

"Look, I'm a bad risk for friendship. I didn't come here today for the pleasure of seeing you. I—I came because I need a thousand pounds and you're the only man I could think of who could help me get it."

McAndrew showed no surprise. He stared into his glass and said, "Then I'm glad you did come to me, Renn. A thousand pounds is little enough to ask of a man whose life you saved. I'll write you a check for it before you go. Now, will you relax and enjoy your drink."

It was so simple, so bland and casual, that it took my breath away. And yet I had not, even then, the grace to accept and be done with it. I talked on, brashly, foolishly.

"But I don't want it that way."

"How do you want it then?"

"I want to tell you first why I need it."

"That's not necessary."

"Just the same I want to tell you."

And I told him. I told him of Jeannette and myself and our island in the sun. I told him of the old coin and the old ship from which I believed it had come. I told him of Manny Mannix and my final folly at Manny's tables and my ignominious exit from the university. I poured it out in an orgy of self-flagellation, and when I had finished I felt suddenly empty and tired.

McAndrew didn't say a word. He got up and refilled my glass and handed it to me.

"Drink it up, man. It'll make you feel better."

I grinned sourly. "That's an old wives' tale. I've tried. It doesn't work."

McAndrew smiled and clapped a friendly hand on my shoulder.

"You've been drinking in the wrong company, that's all. If you'd had sense enough to come to me in the first place . . ."

We drank. I put down the glass carefully and, just as carefully, I explained to him.

"Mac, I want money, yes. I want it more than I can say, for more reasons than I can explain, but I don't want your money."

"Call it a loan then, to be paid when you raise your treasure ship."

"No, Mac. Not a loan either. I want it to be my money. If I find what I'm looking for, I want it to be mine, too. . . . I don't know if I can make you understand this. But I want something like you have here . . . your land, your horses, your own life. That's what I want from my treasure ship. A place of my own, a life of my own."

"Would you be happy in it? Without her?"

"I don't know. But if I can't have Jeannette, I want the other things. The things I hoped she would share with me. Can you understand that?"

"Yes, I can. But I don't see what you mean about the money."

"Then I'll tell you. Call me crazy, if you like. But this is how I want it. You race horses. You race winners. When you have a good one coming up, at a good price, tens or better, I want you to tell me. I want you to give me the same chance as the stable, to lay my money on it. It's only a hundred. It won't kill the market . . . and if it comes home, I'll have my stake and a small revenge on the bookies. That's all I want."

McAndrew stared at me in amazement.

"Renn, you're crazy. Every race is a gamble. Every horse is a gamble. The best horse in the world can lose. What then?"

"Then I'll go to Queensland and cut cane or get myself a job as shearer's cook. All I ask is the chance, Mac, the same chance that the stable has. A good horse trying to win."

"But if it loses, you lose everything."

"I lose a hundred pounds. That isn't everything."

"It's everything you have. My way, you could have the money without risk, without obligation."

"That way I lose the one thing I still have—independence."

There was a long, long minute while McAndrew considered the proposition. It was plain that it was distasteful to him. By all rules I was making a damn fool of myself. I was also cheating a gentle, good man of the chance to repay a debt with generosity. Had I known then what I know now I should have taken his check and kissed the hand that offered it to me. But I was a cross-grained historian who refused to learn the lessons of history, so I let McAndrew piece out the answer himself. He gave it to me quietly, without restraint.

"All right, Renn. If you would let me give you the money, or even lend it to you, you'd make me very happy. You won't. I think I understand why. Black Bowman is running in the third at Randwick tomorrow. He'll open at twelves and start somewhere about threes. So get your money on early. We think he'll win. If he doesn't, it won't be our fault or his. I wish you luck."

I held out my hand. He took it. And before he released it, he said to me, "You've had a stormy passage, Renn. It isn't over yet. But there's a safe landfall at McAndrew's. Remember that."

"I'll remember it. I'm more grateful than I can say. But I'm sailing my own course, and if I don't make harbour it'll be no one's fault but my own."

I left him then and walked down the long drive to the highway. Across the far side of a paddock a black stallion picked up his heels and set off at a gallop round the perimeter. For a fleeting moment I thought it was Black Bowman. But then I remembered Black Bowman would be in his stall by now, resting his strength for the third race at Randwick.

I arrived at the course in the middle of the second race. The crowds were roaring as the favourite was being beaten in a canter by a rank outsider from the country. The bookies' ring was deserted, as I knew it would be, and I took up my position near the rails of the enclosure, where the big men laid the odds to big money and a hundred-pound bet wouldn't send the market tumbling.

It's a touchy business when the stable is set for a strike. There are thousands of pounds to invest before the odds tumble to threes or worse, and every bookmaker in the ring is warned to close the betting before the betting closes on him. There are a dozen commission men in the ring, each with the stable's money in his pocket, and the pencillers are busy totting up the risks and the runners watch beady-eyed for the familiar faces of these men who make a business out of beating the books for owners and trainers and the big gambling syndicates. I had to beat the bookies and the commissioners both. I had to place my bet as soon as the odds were called. So I took up my position near the stand of Bennie Armstrong, the biggest bookie on the course, and waited.

A groan went up as the outsider came home, lengths ahead of the field. Two minutes later the betting opened on the third race.

On Australian courses the odds are displayed on every

bookmaker's board and changes are made on numbered
rollers rather like markers in a billiard saloon. Bennie
Armstrong showed twelve to one against Black Bowman.
Five yards away a colleague was offering fourteen. I
calculated the time it would take me to push through the
crowd and take the longer odds. It wasn't worth the risk.
The commissioners would be spreading their money and
the odds might tumble in thirty seconds. I turned to
Bennie, held up a bundle of five-pound notes and called
my bet.

"Twelve hundred to a hundred, Black Bowman. . . ."

Bennie shot me a quick glance. His clerk grabbed my
money, counted swiftly and stuffed it in his bag; he
nodded to Bennie, who pencilled a ticket and thrust it at
me.

"You're on. Twelve hundred to a hundred."

Then he twisted the roller on his board and the odds
were down to ten. I glanced across at the other board.
Eights! I had been lucky. The stable money was going on
now . . . and before the barrier went up Black Bowman would be offering at evens.

I put the ticket in my wallet and walked across to the
grandstand to find myself a seat. My mouth was dry and
my stomach was knotted with excitement. I needed a
drink badly, but the thought of the bar with its clamour
of voices and its smell of spilt liquor turned me sick. I
swallowed and licked my lips to moisten them and wiped
the clamminess from my hands, then mounted the steps
near the broadcasting booth on the main stand.

It was a clear day, but there was no heat in the sun.
The women on the lawns seemed touched with the
drabness of autumn. The flower beds lacked colour and
the crowd was thinner than usual. But the track was firm
and the air was still and that was enough for me. I saw
the strappers lead the horses into the enclosure. I
watched the small men in bright silks carrying their
saddles to the scales. I saw the purple and gold of the

McAndrew stable and my heart beat a little faster. McAndrew had Minsky riding for him, and if God had made a horse to win the mile and a half he would have picked Minsky to ride him.

They were saddling up now. Minsky and McAndrew and McAndrew's trainer were talking together. They stood in the relaxed attitudes of men who know their business, who know that they have done all that can be done and that from this point everything depends on the horse and jockey and God Almighty.

The trainer hefted Minsky into the saddle. He tried the girth and tightened the leathers. Then Minsky reached down and McAndrew reached up and they clasped hands along the sleek, rippling shoulder of Black Bowman. It was an odd, intimate little ritual in which I had no part. Black Bowman was carrying my money and my future, but I had no part in him, or he in me. If he won, it would be because McAndrew had bred him and McAndrew's men had trained him and a gnome in the McAndrew silks crouched over his neck. I was a punter, and a punter is a parasite on the pelt of a noble horse.

Now the clerk of the course was leading them out onto the track. His thick-barrelled hunter made a laughable contrast with the fine, nervous lines of the thoroughbreds. Minsky was taking the Bowman at a gentle walk and the black stallion was stepping as daintily as a ballerina. He started and sidestepped as a big bay passed him in a warming canter, but Minsky quietened him and tightened the reins a fraction. A good man, Minsky, a wise old Jehu. I was glad my money was riding with him.

Black Bowman was drawn number ten at the barrier. It was a good position in the middle of the field. They couldn't pin him against the rails or jostle him on the turns, and if Minsky could get him away to a clean start, he could run freely with the field until they came to the last five furlongs that make proof of a horse's muscle and heart and of his jockey's cunning and skill.

The air was full of a metallic buzzing as the commentator called the positions and tried to convey to his unseen audience the small confusion at the barrier. I couldn't distinguish the words, but I raised the glasses and saw Black Bowman standing steady at the tapes while the starter moved the last three mounts into line. One was in and the other two were turning away. The jockeys pulled them round and faced them in again. They moved forward. The tapes went up. The crowd roared. They were racing. . . .

I saw the flash of purple and gold as Minsky moved out to a clean start. Then I lost him in the press of horses that settled down behind the pacemakers for the first half mile.

A roan gelding and a big grey were out in front. There was a straggle of bad starters coasting along for the exercise. But the winner was somewhere in the tight bunch in the middle of the field, and nobody could begin to guess at him till they thinned out at the three-quarter mile and the boys who were riding to win nosed up into position.

The roan dropped out at the mile, and at the seven the grey was in the lead, but dropping back into the field. By the time they hit the five the bunch was split in two, and I saw Minsky and Black Bowman striding comfortably at the tail of the first eight horses. At the half mile there were still eight, but two were falling back and Black Bowman was still tailing the first half dozen. Minsky was riding a copybook race until they turned into the straight. Then my heart sank. The favourite moved across to the rails. Three more riders moved abreast and Black Bowman was a length behind the fourth. I tried to focus on him, but the horse ahead of him blocked my view. I saw the favourite's rider take to his whip. I saw the first three horses lengthen strides as the riders crouched forward in their irons. If the Bowman didn't move now, he was finished and so was I.

Then I saw. And the crowd saw. And we leapt to our feet and roared. Minsky had moved Black Bowman to the outside. He was four lengths behind the leader. But he was out of the saddle, cramped by his skinny knees right up on the shoulders of Black Bowman. His head was down behind the rear of his mount, he was giving him rein, as much as he wanted, and the big stallion was stretching out. Three lengths—two—then he was level with the leader. Then Minsky laid the whip across his flank so lightly that you wondered that he felt it, and the Bowman leapt forward to win by a length and a half.

I waited to see the numbers go up. I waited till correct weight had been signalled. I patted my pocket to assure myself that the bookie's ticket was safe. Then I walked from the course and caught a taxi to my lodgings. I was richer by twelve hundred pounds. I wondered that I felt so little excited by it.

On Monday morning I went to the settling at Tattersalls Club. Bennie Armstrong paid, as he always did, with a smile and an invitation to do more business with him.

I was counting the crisp new notes and stuffing them into a briefcase when Manny Mannix slapped me on the shoulder.

"Looks like you had a good day, Commander."

I nodded briefly and said, "Yes, quite good."

"More than a grand in that little lot," said Manny.

I stowed the last of the notes in the briefcase and snapped the catch.

"That's right, Manny. More than a grand."

Manny grinned shrewdly.

"So now you've got your stake, eh, Commander?"

"As you say, Manny, I've got my stake."

He smiled then—the old, hearty, no-hard-feelings smile—and held out his hand.

"I guess you had it coming, Commander. I wish you luck."

I ignored his hand and looked him full in the eyes.

"You're a bastard, Manny," I said softly.

Then I tucked the briefcase under my arm and walked out of the club.

That was the second mistake I made. Call another man a bastard and he'll punch you on the nose. But a man like Manny wants to show you how much of a bastard he really can be.

Chapter Four

My money was stowed in the bank. My seat was booked on the aircraft. There was a letter in the post to the Lands Department of the Queensland Government telling them of my arrival to negotiate the purchase or lease of an inner-reef island noted thus and thus in the surveys. My gear was packed and my rent was paid. I took a ferry ride up the Lane Cove to talk to Nino Ferrari.

Nino is a Genoese, a spare, stringy brown man with crow's feet at the corners of his eyes. Nino had been a frogman with Mussolini's navy and Nino had sent more than a few thousand tons of Allied shipping to the bottom of the Mediterranean.

A migrant now, he ran a small waterfront factory fabricating diving gear for the navy and the spearfishermen and the boys who have fallen under the spell of the blue deeps. His work is precise, reliable. His knowledge of deep-water skindiving is encyclopedic.

I told him what I wanted—diving gear and cylinders. He questioned me gravely.

"This is for pleasure, Signor Lundigan—or business?"

"Does it make any difference, Nino?"

"Sì, sì . . . it makes a great deal of difference."

"Why?"

Nino shrugged and spread his hands in deprecation.

"Why? I will tell you why. You buy this thing for pleasure, you will find yourself a nice interesting rock hole twenty feet deep maybe and you will play for hours without much danger. You will take a holiday in the sun and go down and look at the coral—spear fish maybe . . . and that is that. You are careful of the sharks, you observe a few simple rules and no harm can come to you. But for business . . ."

He broke off. I waited a moment, then prompted him gently.

"For business, Nino?"

"For business, my friend, you need training."

"I haven't time."

"Then you will probably kill yourself, very soon."

That stopped me in my tracks. Nino wasn't fooling. Nino was a professional. Nino had nothing to lose by telling me the truth. I asked myself whether I had anything to lose by telling Nino the truth. His cool, level eyes answered that I had not. So I told him.

"I'm looking for a ship, Nino."

To Nino this was a commonplace. He nodded soberly.

"Salvage?"

"Treasure."

Nino's weathered face relaxed into a smile. "You know where this ship is?"

"I know where it should be. I have to find it first."

"Where do you expect to find it?"

I told him. I told him what I believed had happened to the *Doña Lucia*. I plotted her course. I showed him how I pictured her end . . . foundering on the outer reef of the Island of the Twin Horns.

Nino listened carefully, nodding approval of my historian's logic. When I had finished he reached for a pencil and a draftsman's pad and began to question me.

"First you will tell me what sort of island this is. Is it an atoll?"

"No. It's a mainland island. A hump of ironstone and

earth with cliffs on one side and a strip of beach on the other. The coral reef has grown round it."

"All around it?"

"That's what the surveys show. But there is a channel. I found it years ago."

Nino sketched rapidly on the pad. He showed the elevation of an island . . . a small mountain heaving up above water level. He showed a long shelf of sand fringed with ragged coral. And beyond the coral a shorter shelf, then a steep drop into deep water. Then he shoved the sketch in front of me.

"It is something like that, perhaps?"

"Very like that."

"Good."

He took up the pencil again and began to make a picture that grew as he talked.

"There are two things that could have happened to your ship. The first: she drives onto the reef in moderate weather. She is holed. She founders. She settles here . . . sliding down the shelf into the deep water. . . . How deep water . . . How deep would you say it is here?"

"I don't know. That is the first thing I have to find out."

Nino nodded. "It is also the most dangerous thing. But we shall return to that. If it is not too deep and if the ship is not already eaten by the coral, then you may have a chance. But . . . if the second thing happened . . . if she foundered in a storm . . . she would have been battered to pieces by the surf. Then, I tell you now, you have not one chance in a million. Her timber would have been shattered, her treasure chests, too, perhaps . . . but even if they were not, they would have sunk to the bottom and two hundred years of coral growth would have devoured them . . . and you will never find them—not till judgment day."

Nino raised his head from the drawing. His frank eyes searched my face.

I put the question to him bluntly.

"If you were in my place, Nino, what would you do?"
He smiled and shook his head.

"If I were in your place, with the experience I have now, I would forget all about the treasure ship and save my money. But . . . if I were you, as you are now, with a dream in your heart and a few pounds in your pocket . . . I would go and look for it."

I grinned at that. The tension between us relaxed. We settled down to talk of practical matters.

"First," said Nino briefly, "you will buy yourself a marine survey map. You will note the depth of the water off this shelf. If it is no more than twenty fathoms . . . then you have a chance. A man can train himself to be comfortable and to work at that depth, provided he observes the decompression tables. Below it . . . no. After that there is the zone of rapture, where men get drunk on the nitrogen in their bodies . . . where every movement is a danger, even to the experienced. You understand enough of this business to know what I mean."

I nodded agreement. I knew the terrors of the bends, when free nitrogen explodes like champagne in the joints and vertebrae and the careless or luckless diver is twisted into fantastic contortions. I had read of the strange, deathly rapture that comes to men in the blue zone, that urges them to talk to the fishes, to rip off their masks, to dance strange sarabands while death waits grinning in the underwater twilight.

Nino returned to his interrogation.

"You realize that you cannot do this thing alone?"
"I shan't be alone. I'll have a . . . a friend with me."
"No lung diver?"
"No . . . a skindiver. An old hand from the trochus luggers. He's a Gilbert Islander. Worked with the Japanese. He's used to deep waters."

"So . . ." Nino pursed his lips. "He will dive with you. But he will not be able to work with you."

"That's the way I want it, Nino. I'll work alone."

He shrugged. "It is your life. I simply tell you the risks."

"I want to know them."

"Then I repeat that you will need training."

"Can I train myself?"

"Ye-es. I will give you a set of rules and exercises. You will practice them daily, rigidly, increasing the dives each day, observing the stages for decompression. You will on no account deviate from the exercises or the directions. Is that understood? Your life will depend on that. This is a new world that you are entering. You must make friends with it—or perish."

I knew that I was foolish not to accept Nino's offer of a training course before I left for my island. But the black devils were at my back, goading. It was up stakes and away, for me, before the dream faded and the sour taste of disillusion settled on my tongue. Nino understood, I think, but he could not approve my folly.

He showed me the equipment, taught me how to maintain its simple mechanism. He put it on me and took me down in a series of short test dives in the rock pool below his workshop.

Then we dressed again and, while we sat over a glass of Chianti in his workshop, Nino listed the items with which he would have to supply me: the lung itself, goggles with safety glass, a weighted belt, flippers, cylinders of compressed air . . .

"Mother of God!" Nino swore quietly. "I am a fool. I had forgotten!"

"What, Nino?"

"This island of yours. Is it far from the mainland?"

"Fifteen miles, more or less. Why?"

"Is there a town nearby?"

"Yes, but once I've bought my stores and moved out, I

don't want to go back. It's a small town. Visitors are a curiosity. Tourists make talk among the locals. That could be bad. But what's the fuss about?"

"This." Nino slapped his hand on the metal air bottle. "You wear two of these. You have enough air for an hour and a half under water. But they have to be refilled, and that needs a three-stage compressor, which is heavy equipment. Probably there is not such a machine even in your town."

It was my turn to swear. I swore . . . competently. "What's the alternative?"

"There is none. I will sell you twenty bottles, which is nearly all my stock. You will have to freight them to your island. That will give you enough for fifteen hours under water. After that you will have to send them to Brisbane to be refilled."

Twenty air bottles at seven pounds each was a hundred and forty pounds—plus air freight. When I left Nino's I would be two hundred and eighty pounds poorer and all I would have would be fifteen hours to find my treasure ship. On the other hand, if I didn't find it in fifteen hours I would never find it.

Nothing to do but pay with good grace and hope that my money would turn to yellow gold, stamped with the head of His Most Catholic Majesty of Spain.

We closed the deal. We talked of technicalities. Then, when the wine was finished and I stood up to leave, Nino Ferrari laid his hand on my shoulder. There was more than a hint of irony in his smile, but whether the irony was directed at me or at himself I could not tell.

"Signor Lundigan," he said, "I will tell you something. When I was diving first round the Mediterranean, you could walk into any bar and meet a man—half a dozen men—who knew about a treasure ship waiting to be raised. In all my life I never met one who had brought up more than a few shards of pottery or a piece of marble or a bronze figurine. And yet you know, and I know, that the treasures of Greece and Rome and Byzantium lie still on the continental shelf. And if you ask me why I tell you this, it is to say to go, go, dive for your ship. Find her if you can. And even if you fail you will have done what the heart demands . . . and that is a more precious thing than all the gold of the King of Spain."

Nino Ferrari is a Genoese. Genoa is a fine, bright adventurous town with a statue of Christopher Columbus in the public square. The craggy old visionary would have been proud of Nino Ferrari. I know that Nino Ferrari made me, for a brief while, proud of myself.

The gentleman in the Lands Department was cheerful and courteous—and quite convinced that I was a lunatic. He pointed out that the Queensland Government was disinclined to alienate any more offshore islands but would be happy to lease my island for ten years or twenty or ninety-nine if I really wanted it so long. He made it clear that no man in his right mind would want a place like that for more than ten minutes. There was no water and no channel through the reef. When I told him there was both water and a channel, he clucked dubiously and asked me to send information on both to the Chief Surveyor—that is if I still wanted to become a tenant of the Crown.

I did want to. I wanted it even more when I discovered that the leasehold would cost me only twenty pounds a year and that I could secure my base of operations without paying out a large slice of hard-won capital.

The lease was drawn, attested, stamped and lodged with the Registrar-General, and Renn Lundigan, Esq., became a tenant of Her Majesty's Government with rights to free and undisturbed possession of a green island with a white beach and a coral reef, fifteen miles off the coast of Queensland.

The whole transaction was so simple, so obviously trivial, that I quite forgot one important fact. To sign, seal, stamp and deliver a document is a legal act, irrefutable as the shorthand of the recording angel—and a damn sight more public. But of this I had no slightest thought as I tucked the copies in my pocket along with my letter of credit and the consignment notes from Nino Ferrari and walked in the raw sunlight towards the freight office of the airline.

My equipment was waiting for me, packed in three wooden crates. I was faced immediately with the problem of getting them out to my island. They could be taken by air up the coast, railed to the small town opposite the island and then taken out by launch. But this did not suit me at all. There was the risk of delay and damage. There was the even greater risk of gossip and unwelcome interest when such bulky stores were shipped out to an island where even the tourists could not be landed for their picnics and their paddles round the Barrier Reef.

Cautiously, I discussed the problem with the freight clerk.

He told me there was a biweekly flying boat which served the tourist islands in Whitsunday Passage. My packages could be landed on one of these. I could collect them in my launch. He presumed I had a launch. I told him I had—which wasn't strictly true. I hoped to have a launch. But I had to find one first and then buy it at my price. I paid the stiff freight bill, signed insurance papers and accepted his personal assurance that my crates would be available for collection any time after Thursday—provided the weather was right and the engine didn't fall out of the ancient Catalina.

Then I bought a ticket for a northbound flight the following afternoon and walked round to Lennon's Hotel to buy myself a drink.

July is the tourist season in Brisbane. The sun has moved north from Capricorn to Cancer. The rains are over and the sky is blue and the air has a crispness that is worth a fortune to the land sharks and the publicans and the keepers of guesthouses and the owners of furnished flats from Southport to Caloundra.

The wealthy move north from Melbourne and Sydney. The playboys flourish their bankrolls and the playgirls peddle their charms. The social weeklies send in their spies, and the cameramen have a field day with the mannequins from the rag houses. You can't get a room for love, though you may get one for money—big money. The tourist islands are packed and the rotogravures turn out colour pages and special supplements on the Riviera of the South Pacific and the Waikiki of the near north.

The shrewd, drawling businessmen in tropic suits smile over their drinks in Lennon's bar and add another thousand to the price of a hundred feet of sand hills in the sucker belt.

I was a stranger among them. They would be friendly to me as they always are to southerners, but I would still be an outlander.

I moved from the bar into the lounge and toyed with a mug of beer while I watched the tourists staging through to the reef islands north or the bikini parade south.

I envied them their freedom and their small or great opulence. True, they had no islands of their own. True, they had neither hope nor thought of bullion chests among the coral branches. But they had no devils on their shoulders either, no goading imps thrusting them out into lonely sea roads to desolate landfalls under the cold moon. They had no compulsion to dive into deep waters, to keep company with painted monstrosities in the forests under the sea. I envied them—but envy is a dangerous vice and self-pity is a more dangerous one still. I had risked too much and lost too much and won my stake too painfully to indulge myself again.

I had just made up my mind to finish my drink and take myself to a theater, when I saw her.

A waiter in a silk shirt and a red cummerbund was showing her to a table under the palms. He was giving her the treatment reserved for the known and the favoured guest. He added a little something of his own, because he was young and she was beautiful—and too careful to show that the beauty was cracking at the seams.

He bent close to her as he drew out the chair. She smiled at him over her bare shoulder and gave her order with the practiced gesture of the mannequin. When she raised her hand, I heard the rattle of her bracelets and saw the dull-gold flash of my Spanish piece.

It was Manny Mannix's girl, the model with the shrewd eyes and the drooping mouth, the girl who had seen me busted at the tables and boosted into the street when I was too drunk to care.

I felt a small cold hand tighten round my heart. If his girl was here, Manny must be here; and Manny was a carrion bird forever circling round a kill.

Then I lit a cigarette and told myself I was a fool. The girl was here alone. She wasn't Manny's girl anymore. She had been paid off as the others had been paid off and she had come north to the gold coast to invest her winnings in a new man with a promising bank balance.

The waiter brought her drink. She paid for it. That was a good sign. Girls like this one never paid for their drinks if they had someone else to pay for them. I saw the coins flicker as she raised her glass to drink, delicately, self-consciously, like a trained animal. Then I had a sudden foolish idea. It restored my confidence and good humour like a drug.

I stubbed out my cigarette and walked across to the quiet corner under the palms. She saw me coming over the last ten paces, but her eyes were blank and her lips held no hint of welcome.

I bent over the table, smiled my little rueful smile and said, "Remember me?"

"I remember you."

Her voice had changed as little as her face. It was still flat, sulky, unlovable.

"Mind if I sit down?"

"No."

"Thanks."

I sat down. She finished her drink and pushed the glass towards me. The gesture was a patent insult.

"You can buy me another if you like."

"You mean if I can aford it."

"Oh, I know you can—Manny told me you were in the money."

Again the small, cold fingers crisped round my heart, but I managed a grin and the words came flatly enough.

"Trust Manny. He's a clever boy."

"He doesn't like you very much, Commander."

"It's a mutual feeling."

She blew a cloud of smoke full in my face and handed me the terse little tag, "That makes three of us, Commander."

"Meaning what?"

"I don't like Manny, either."

"I thought he was with you."

"No. Manny has other interests. This one's a brunette."

I said I was sorry to hear it. I was about to say that men who treated girls the way Manny treated girls were no kind of men at all. She cut off my little philippic with a gamin gesture.

"Save it, Commander. You don't like me. I don't like you. Let's not make pretty speeches. You know Manny gave me your coin?"

She held out her wrist so that the old piece dangled provocatively under my nose.

"Yes. He told me he'd give it to you."

For the first time she smiled. She moistened her lips with a small darting tongue. Her eyes were alight with malicious amusement.

"Like to have it back?"

"Yes."

"How much will you pay?"

"Thirty pounds. That's what Manny gave me for it."

"Make it fifty, Commander, and you can have the rest of the junk as well."

I took out my wallet, counted out ten five-pound notes and laid them on the table without a word. She unclasped the bracelet and tossed it across to me, then picked up the notes and stuffed them into her handbag.

"Thanks," she said flatly. "I was down to my last fiver. Now you can buy me that drink."

I took out a ten-shilling note and put it carefully under the ashtray. Then I stood up.

"I'm sorry. I'm moving out of town. You'd do better with the tourist traffic. They're playing. I'm working."

It sounded cheap and it was cheap. Manny Mannix himself couldn't have made it any dirtier. I tried to find grace enough and words to make an apology.

"I—I'm sorry. I shouldn't have said that."

She shrugged and reached for her compact.

"I'm used to it. There's one thing, Commander . . ."

"Yes?"

"You overpaid me for the bracelet. To make up the difference, I'll tell you something."

"Well . . . ?"

"Manny told me you've got something he wants."

"That's the way Manny lives—wanting what someone else has."

"This time he swears he's going to get it."

"He'll have to find me first and he'll be a long time looking. And even if he does find me . . ."

I was moving away as I spoke, but she stopped me in my tracks.

"When he finds you, Commander . . . when he finds you, he's going to kill you."

Chapter Five

The aircraft levelled out at eight thousand feet and through the starboard port I could see its shadow darting like a bird across the green carpet of the hinterland.

Eastward was the sea and the reef and the jade islands. Westward, far beyond our view, were the parched brown plains of the cattle country. Below us was the lush coastal belt, where the monsoons watered the low hills and filled the swamps, where the ibis gathered and the brolgas made their mysterious bird ballet on the mud flats.

Here were the cane fields and the pineapple plantations and the groves of papaws and the spreading mango trees. Here were the lush pastures of the milking herds. Here were the lean, slow-spoken men of the north—the cane cutters, the mill hands, the drovers who walk with the lounging roll of saddle-bred men. Here are the sad, lost people bred from the old race and the new, whose blood is tinctured with the blood of China and Japan and the Gilberts and the Spice Islands.

Here the houses were built on stilts so that the wind could blow all about them and cool them after the steaming lazy days. Here was the riot of bougainvillaea over creaking veranda posts and galvanized roofs. Here men were rich because they had time to spend. Here men were poor indeed if they could not find a friend among the open-handed people of the Queen's own land. Here there was work for any man who cared to put his hand to it. And if he cared for nothing but to nibble a grass twig on the veranda steps, why, he might do that, too, and be damned to the rest of you.

To me, Renn Lundigan, riding high between a blue heaven and a green earth, there came a curious calm, a sense of release, as if a navel cord had been cut and I were born into a new, free world, remote from danger, emptied of memory, beyond the ache of desire and the pain of loss.

I was headed for Bowen—a small harbour town where the tropic lushness covers the scars of the cyclones and the sudden storms. From Bowen I must travel south again, doubling back on my tracks for fifty miles. At first sight this might have seemed a folly, since the aircraft would have set me down at my destination without the fatigue of three hours on the antique railway service. But this did not suit my book at all.

My town was smaller even than Bowen. A stranger arriving by air is either a tourist or a commerical traveller. As such, he is an object of courteous but lively interest. His every movement is a subject of gossip among the fraternity in the bar or the lounges under the shopfront verandas.

Come in by train, dusty, crumpled, irritable, and they are prepared to take you at any value you care to set—stock inspector, commission agent, fisheries man, or a clerk from one of the sugar mills. If you pay your score and don't talk too loudly or spend too much and show some knowledge of the local scene, they'll leave you to your own devices and forget the questions they meant to ask you, because it's too hot to remember.

My knowledge of the local scene was pitifully inadequate, but I was counting on Johnny to fill in the gaps for me.

His full name was Johnny Akimoto. He was the son of

a Japanese trochus diver and a Gilbertese woman. The mother's blood was stronger, and except for a curious greyness of complexion and an Oriental tightness about the eyes and cheekbones, Johnny would have passed for a full-blooded islander. Ever since the blackbirding days, when island men were shanghaied for work on the cane fields, these curious racial mixtures have been found all along the Queensland coast.

Johnny himself had worked the trochus luggers. He had sailed with the pearlers and dived on the deep beds. But when the war came and there was no more work for a skindiver, Johnny became an odd-job man. He had been houseboy to the Americans, roustabout on a tourist island, engine hand on a fishing boat, truck driver for a local contracter. Everybody knew Johnny. Everybody liked him, and when Jeannette and I had run ashore in cyclone weather, it was Johnny who mended our sails and repaired our sheathing and painted the hull and read us wise lectures on the offshore weather in the bad season.

It was Johnny who had helped me trace the course of the Acapulco galleons. When I had told him of our first wild hopes of the *Doña Lucia*, he had nodded approval and promised that one day he would dive with me round the reef of the Island of the Twin Horns. A wise, quiet man, Johnny Akimoto. A gentle, loyal man. A lonely, lost man among the friendly people of the coast.

I thought of Johnny as the plane thrust northward. I dozed and dreamt of Manny Mannix and the girl who had sold me back my coin for fifty pounds. I woke to find the hostess at my shoulder warning me to fasten my seat belt. The plane banked sharply over a stretch of blue water. I closed my eyes, and when I opened them again I saw a bellying wind sock and a huddle of iron-roofed sheds. We were coming in to land.

We sweltered in the dusty waiting room while they unloaded our baggage. It was midafternoon and the sea

breeze would not come for another hour. I found myself
in conversation with a tubby fellow in an alpaca suit. He
told me he was a retired bank manager. He told me he
was going to join his wife and daughter on a luxury island
offshore from Bowen. He told me how much it was going
to cost him. He told me how little he was going to enjoy
it. He told me how the heat gave him rashes and the cold
gave him bronchitis. He told me his golf handicap and
his ambition to raise prize dahlias. He told me . . .

"Mr. Renn Lundigan?"

The airport clerk was at my elbow.

"That's right."

"Telegram for you, sir. Came in just before you
landed."

He handed me a buff envelope with a red border. It
was franked "Urgent." I slit the envelope and unfolded
the message form. The office of origin was Brisbane. The
filing time was half an hour after midday. The message
was brief and hearty as a handshake:

GOOD FISHING COMMANDER STOP BE SEEING YOU STOP

And it was signed "Manny Mannix."

I crumpled the paper and thrust it into my pocket.
The tubby bank manager looked at me curiously. He
wanted to get on with his story. I turned away and left
him gaping. I felt suddenly sick and lonelier than I had
ever been since Jeannette was taken from me. I wanted
very much to talk to Johnny Akimoto.

The train journey was a slow torment. I was hot,
dusty, beset with flies and badgered to insanity by a pair
of small boys who whined continuously for sweets and
drinks while their mother nagged vainly for peace.

We stopped at every siding while the guard exchanged
news with the station staff. We were shunted onto a loop
and waited three-quarters of an hour for the northbound

train to go through. The green country which had seemed so rich and desirable from the air was now in the grip of a drooping misery which matched my own depression. The friendly people of the north were a drab and garrulous race. Their children were monsters. Their transport service was a primitive horror. Their greetings were an intrusion on my privacy. Their gifts of newspapers and fruit and lemonade were a presumption not to be borne. By the time the journey was over they had written me down as a cross-grained boor. Looking back, I find I agree with them.

Manny's telegram had shocked me deeply. The first blind rage passed quickly and then fear took hold of me. I did not believe for a moment that Manny's threat to kill me was anything more than a boast to impress a woman. But the fear remained—fear of losing something I did not yet possess, but which I had struggled and schemed and gambled to attain.

More than this, I knew the power that lay in Manny's hands. Money power. Power to buy a man here and a piece of information there. Power to plan his moves like a chess game, to check me here and circumvent me there, to match any move of mine with another, shrewder, swifter and more effective. I thought of the three crates of equipment in the airways office at Brisbane and wondered if he could do anything to divert them.

I remembered that Manny could pay for a charter flight and might even now be waiting to greet me at the hotel. I wondered what I would do if he were.

But he wasn't. I was the only guest. I could have the best bedroom with the iron bedstead and the big mosquito net and the cracked ewer and basin. I could have free use of the single bathroom and walk fifty yards to the lavatory in the yard. I could drink alone in the commercial room. I could rise at seven-thirty and breakfast alone at eight. I could accept mine host's wheezy invitation and join the mill hands and the fishermen telling bawdy stories in the bar. They were good boys. They'd make me very welcome. But I wanted none of that. I wanted a shower and a drink and a meal— and then I wanted to see Johnny Akimoto.

I found him where I had found him the first time. In a small slab hut with the bush at its back and the sand dunes in front. The coral paths were raked clean every day. There was a trailing of bougainvillaea and a hibiscus tree and a border of sweet gardenia, and a tall frangipani whose naked branches thrust out like the symbols of some ancient phallic cult.

A kerosene lamp hung on a nail in the door jamb, and Johnny was sitting on a packing case splicing hooks on a trawl line. He wore a hibiscus flower in his frizzy hair and his only clothing was a pair of denim shorts.

He looked up sharply when he heard my footfall and his face broke into a gleaming smile of surprise and welcome.

He came to me, hand outstretched.

"Renboss!"

"That's right, Johnny. Renboss."

It was the old name, from the old happy time. It brought me very near to tears. Johnny pumped my hand and patted my back and made me sit down on another packing case which he dragged out of the shadows into the small circle of light.

"What brings you here, Renboss? You staying long? How are things with you? You are well? You look tired, but that's the travelling, eh?"

The questions came tumbling out in Johnny's precise Mission English, and all the time he was looking into my face, searching like an anxious mother for the truth about a child.

I told him the truth.

"I came to see you, Johnny."

"Me? That's nice, Renboss. I often thought about you . . . and the missy."

"The missy is dead, Johnny."

"Oh, no. When?" His mild eyes were full of sympathy.

"A long time go, Johnny. A long, lonely time."

"You got no other woman?"

"No other woman."

"And you came back here to see Johnny Akimoto. That's good, Renboss. I've got a boat now. A good boat. We go out on the reef, eh? You come out and fish with me, eh? We take a trip together to Thursday Island . . . Moresby, maybe."

"We take a trip, Johnny . . . yes . . . but not to Thursday . . . to my island. . . ."

"Your island?" He looked at me in momentary puzzlement, then he grinned happily. "Oh, yes, I remember. The island of the treasure ship, eh? You say she's your island?"

"I've leased it, Johnny. It's mine. We're going diving for the *Doña Lucia*. I want you to come with me."

Johnny was silent. He turned his hands palm upwards and seemed to study the lines and creases in the flesh. Then after a moment he fished in his pocket for a cigarette and handed one to me. We lit up. We smoked for a few moments, listening to the wash of the water and the searching voice of the wind.

Then Johnny spoke, quietly, professionally.

"To do a thing like this, Renboss, you need a boat."

"I've got money to buy one, Johnny."

"You need a diver and equipment."

"We skindive, Johnny. We use diving gear."

"You have dived before, Renboss?"

"A little. A practice dive or two . . . no more."

"Then you have to learn much before you make a working diver."

"That I want you to teach me, Johnny. Also, I have a

list of exercises from the man who made the diving gear. He says I can train myself to work in twenty fathoms."

"Twenty fathoms!" Johnny was shocked. "Too deep, Renboss . . . too deep for skindives. . . ."

"It can be done, Johnny. This is not naked diving. A man can breathe down there. . . ."

Johnny shook his head. "This is new to me. I don't like the sound of it."

"Will you come with me, Johnny? Will you help me buy a boat and get stores and—"

"No need to buy a boat," said Johnny quietly. "We use mine. She's lugger-built. Old when I bought her, but I patched her up and she will sail you anywhere. The engine is new. She will make eight, ten knots if you want."

"All right, then, I rent the boat. I pay you wages. You come to the island and work with me. Is that the way you want it?"

Johnny nodded soberly. "That's the way, Renboss. Easy, quick—no trouble. You try to buy a boat around here. They sell you a bad boat for a good price. Or a good boat you can't pay for. This is the Reef, Renboss. A man who does not look after a boat finds the teredo eating it. Then he tries to sell it to someone who doesn't know about teredo . . . you see?"

I saw. I knew the teredo, the small mollusk that bores into the timbers in the warm latitudes, eating a boat as the white ants eat a house. There is only one remedy— sheathe your boat with copper to the waterline or paint her over and over with bronze paint till she has a new skin impervious to the sea worm. The boatmen on the Queensland coast are like the horse copers of Kerry . . . and more than one is a lineal descendant of the same fabulous rascals.

Besides, another thought had occurred to me. Johnny's boat was a lugger, a lolloping, awkward craft if you try to sail her too close to the weather, but a deep-water

boat nonetheless, safe as a bank and comfortable in the
trades. If we raised the treasure chests from the *Doña
Lucia*, the whole find would be treasure trove, the
property of the Crown, and I was at the mercy of the
Crown for whatever payment might be made by way of
reward. But with Johnny's lugger, with Johnny's knowledge of the islands, we could up anchor and head north
until we found a Chinese who would pay notes for
minted gold, or an agent who needed gold to pay for
smuggled guns. It's flourishing business in the Celebes
and in the China Straits, and for gold you can name your
own price and your own currency. I didn't speak the
thought to Johnny. Johnny might not approve. Besides,
there would be time enough later.

Johnny smoked quietly, weighing his next question.
His face was in shadow, but his eyes were intent on my
face.

"Renboss, you are afraid of something. What is it?"

"I'm coming to that, Johnny. It's a long story."

"If we are to work together, Renboss, I should know
the story."

I told him. I told him about Manny Mannix and the
girl in Lennon's Hotel. I told him about the telegram. I
told him how I feared Manny Mannix and the power that
money put into his hands.

Johnny blew smoke rings and watched them drift away
on the eddies of the wind.

"We should get out quickly," he said.

"I'm ready to move whenever you are, Johnny."

"We need stores, first."

"When can you get those?"

"Tomorrow. Stores and a medicine chest. Accidents
can happen on the Reef and in the water."

"I'll make a list of them tonight. There's a chemist in
the town?"

Johnny nodded. "There is a chemist. Better, I think,

you buy the medicines. I will see to the stores. If you start to buy yourself, people will ask questions."

"When can we leave, Johnny?"

"The day after tomorrow . . . first light."

"Not before?"

"No," said Johnny firmly. "What good does it do? We have to make the boat ready. We have to go down to the tourist island to collect your gear. Then we have to sail a lugger through a narrow reef passage. That is daytime work. Silly to risk a boat for no profit."

"But what if Manny comes before we're ready to move?"

"Why should he come?"

"Simple enough, Johnny. The one thing Manny doesn't know is where I'm going. He knows there's an island. He doesn't know its name or its location."

"Don't fool yourself, Renboss," said Johnny gravely. "Don't try to make yourself believe what is not true. You bought this island, didn't you? Like I bought this hut and this little piece of ground."

"I leased it."

"The same thing. You signed papers. The papers are registered with the Government office in Brisbane. Anyone can go in, pay two and sixpence and find out everything he wants about the transaction. You see?"

I couldn't fail to see. It was too simple, pat and final. I was a historian. I could trace the decline of empires and the fall of heroes, but I had forgotten one of the simplest legalities of modern living.

Manny Mannix didn't have to do anything. He just had to wait and then move in for the kill. And all it would cost him was two and sixpence.

I laughed. I couldn't help it. I laughed until hysterical tears ran down my face and the birds nesting in the bush behind the hut began chattering in sudden fright.

Johnny Akimoto stood and watched me with quiet concern. The laughter spent itself in a fit of coughing. I asked him, rather foolishly, for another cigarette. He handed it to me, lit it and then said, "You feel better now, Renboss?"

"I'm all right, Johnny."

"Good. Tomorrow I buy the stores, you see to the medicine chest. I meet you here at three o'clock in the afternoon. We get the stuff on board and make her shipshape before nightfall. We sleep on board and raise anchor at first light."

I took out my wallet and handed Johnny fifty pounds in notes.

"That see you through for the stores?"

"More than plenty, Renboss."

"The rest of the money is in the bank, Johnny. I'll settle with you tomorrow or later, whenever you like."

"You settle when we finish the job, Renboss."

Johnny smiled his rare flashing smile and clapped me on the shoulder.

"And if we don't finish it, Johnny?"

"Then we do like I said the first time. Go north to Thursday, to New Guinea, and maybe catch ourselves some trade, eh? Go home, Renboss, go home and get some sleep. Things always look better when the sun shines in the morning."

"Good night, Johnny."

"Good night, Renboss."

I walked back to the hotel under a sky that was full of stars. I drank with the mill hands in the bar. I don't remember finding my way to bed. I don't remember anything until the raw sun woke me at ten in the morning.

Chapter Six

I crawled painfully out of bed and made my way down to the bathroom to wash the sleep out of my eyes and the stink of liquor off my skin. I dressed slowly, resigned to the thought that it was now too late for breakfast. I packed my bag and paid my bill, declining the offer of a drink on the house in favour of a cup of tea in the kitchen. Then, leaving my bag behind the bar to be collected later, I walked down to the low timber building that was the town's only bank.

The manager was a tall, ruddy man in a fresh linen shirt and starched shorts. When I presented my letter of credit, he greeted me as if I were a millionaire and invited me into his office for yet another cup of tea. His manner cooled considerably and he gave me a sidelong look when I told him I wanted to lodge my letter of credit for safekeeping, and that if I did not return within three months the whole amount of the credit was to be paid to the personal account of Johnny Akimoto. He drew some papers from the drawer of his desk and laid them on the blotter in front of him.

Then he began to quiz me.

"Is there any reason why you should not return in three months, Mr. Lundigan?"

"None that I can think of at this moment, but it's as well to be prepared, don't you think?"

"Of course, but what for, Mr. Lundigan?"

"Accidents do happen, don't they?"

"True enough, but . . ." He realized that he was on the verge of an indiscretion. He stopped short and gave me his practiced, professional smile. "Of course the bank will make any dispositions you wish. You have only to sign the papers and . . . Well, that's all there is to it. I was just curious."

This sort of question and answer could go on indefinitely. I decided there was no harm in telling him at least half of the story. I told him.

"I've leased an island off the coast. I'm a naturalist. I'm making a study of marine life at depths of fifteen and twenty fathoms. I use diving gear. That entails certain risks. I've rented Johnny Akimoto's boat and I'm paying him a weekly wage in addition. If anything happens to me, I want him to be able to claim payment and to have whatever is left over by way of a bonus."

The bank manager relaxed again. He might be dealing with an oddity, but at least I was not the lunatic he at first thought.

The tea came at that moment, and he began to make small talk again. I endured it for a while with reasonable courtesy, because I had a question to put to him.

"Tell me . . . do you know anything about water rights?"

"Water rights?"

His eyebrows went up again.

"Yes, water rights. What rights, if any, has the freeholder or leaseholder of an island over the surrounding waters?"

He thought for a moment and then said, "It is not a question that normally arises. In law as I know it, the holder's land rights extend to the low-water mark, in practice they are presumed to extend to the inner fringes of the reef surrounding the island. You might possibly have an action for trespass, but I think it would be a long and costly business to sustain. In any event, the question is hardly likely to arise, is it?"

"No, I suppose it isn't, but one likes to be sure of these matters."

"Impossible to be sure in this case, I'm afraid, Mr. Lundigan. But"—he spread his hands in a gesture of smiling disparagement—"there is a lot of water and a lot of islands on the reef. Your island is off the tourist tracks anyway. If you make it clear that you want to be private, I don't think you'll be bothered very much."

I couldn't tell him about Manny Mannix, so there wasn't any point in pressing the question. I nodded and smiled and made some fatuous remark about students being odd cattle anyway. Then he handed me the papers to sign.

We finished our tea, we shook hands and I walked out again across the street. Halfway down on the other side was a small single-fronted shop with gold lettering on the window and an old-fashioned glass jar full of coloured water behind the dusty pane.

I walked across and introduced myself to the proprietor. He was young, which was fortunate for me. He was talkative, which was an annoyance, but he accepted my story with more readiness than the bank manager had done and was quite ready to waive the formalities of prescriptions and doctors' signatures when I asked him for Atabrine tablets and penicillin and sulfanilamide. I bought iodine and bandages and aspirin and a small scalpel and had them packed in a small wooden box provided by the garrulous young druggist.

But I was not to escape so easily. Time is at discount in the north, and the most casual customer is expected to make his own contribution to the conversational gambits of the community.

I listened with mild interest to a curtain lecture on the stings of bluebottles and sea urchins and the danger of the dreaded stonefish. I heard, without too much concern, that another naturalist had passed through the town only a fortnight before—a girl, this time, quite young, very attractive according to the young chemist, who, fresh from the university, was no doubt finding the local fillies something less than interesting.

I escaped at last, clutching my little wooden box under my arm, only to find that I had hours yet to kill before I made rendezvous with Johnny Akimoto at his hut behind the sand dunes.

Sudden panic overtook me as I stood on the cracked pavement bubbling with hot tar and saw the rickety town peter out at either end of the single main street. The riot of green, the raw colours of bougainvillaea and poinsettia seemed to close in on me, weigh me down, with their rioting strength. Johnny Akimoto's warning came back to me, and this, added to Nino Ferrari's caution about the dangers of an inexperienced diver, made me afraid and set me cursing my own foolhardiness for embarking, with so little preparation, on a project that scared even the professionals.

The thought of Manny Mannix nagged at me, too. I wondered what he would do next, where I should meet him, what would happen when we came face to face. Then I saw that I was standing opposite the post office.

On an impulse I crossed the street, presented myself at the counter and placed a trunk call to Nino Ferrari. The wilting clerk looked at me as if I had ordered the Eiffel Tower, then he scribbled the number on a slip of paper and told me to wait by the phone booth outside.

I waited. I waited a full hour, and when Nino finally came on the line his voice sounded faint and far away, as if it had been filtered through wet linen. He said, "This is Ferrari. Who is calling?"

"This is Lundigan, Nino—Renn Lundigan."

"So soon? Didn't your stuff arrive?"

"The stuff's all right, Nino. It's being shipped from Brisbane today."

"Then why do you call me?"

"Because I'm scared, Nino."

I thought I heard him chuckle, but I couldn't be sure.

"What are you scared of, my friend?"

"I think I'm crazy, Nino."

He really laughed this time: a full-bellied laugh that came crackling in fantastic distortions over the thousand miles of cable.

"I know you're crazy. There was no need to spend good money to tell me that. Is there anything I can do for you?"

"Yes, Nino, there is. I'm expecting trouble."

"Trouble? What sort of trouble?"

I had to be cautious now. There is no privacy in a public telephone booth in a Queensland country town.

"I told you, Nino, there is someone who doesn't like me."

"You told me, yes. Has anything happened?"

"Not yet, but I want to ask you, if there is trouble, would you come up and help me out?"

There was a long pause. I thought for a moment we had been cut off. Then Nino's voice crackled again over the wire.

"What sort of help do you want? Diving?"

"And other things, too, perhaps. I don't know yet. I can't predict what may happen. I'm just taking out insurance, that's all."

There was another pause. I knew what Nino was thinking. He was a newcomer to this country. He had once been an enemy. If he got into any trouble, it could prejudice his chances of naturalization. I was asking more than I had a right to ask. I knew it, too, but I was too scared to care.

Then Nino spoke. "All right, friend, if you want me, you send for me. I will come on the first plane. You can pay the bills?"

"I'll pay the bills, Nino . . . and thanks."

Nino chuckled. "I'll thank you better if you stay out of trouble and let me run my business."

"I'll try, Nino, but I can't promise it. I'll send you the rest of the story in today's mail. Good-bye for the present and thanks again."

"Good-bye, my friend," said Nino, "and stay out of trouble as long as you can."

The line went dead. I hung up the receiver. I walked back into the post office, bought myself an air letter and scribbled a note to Nino Ferrari.

When I dropped it in the mailbox I felt less lonely and less afraid. There were three of us now. Three men and a good boat and a friendly island. Manny Mannix could do his damnedest. I picked up my little box of medicines and walked down the track to the sand hills to meet Johnny Akimoto.

Johnny's boat was lying a hundred yards offshore, rolling a little in the oily swell. She was ketch-rigged, freshly painted, and her brasswork shone under the loving care of Johnny's hands. Her sails were old but carefully patched. A workmanlike boat run by a good workman. She had a hold amidships and cabin space aft. Her decks were swabbed clean, and her movables were stowed with the sailor's careful precision.

It took us three trips in the dinghy to get the stores aboard, and when we had stowed them and closed the hatch down Johnny busied himself with the small fuel stove in the galley.

I sat on the bunk and talked to him while he worked.

"She's a good boat, Johnny. I like her."

He grinned at me over his shoulder.

"A good boat is like a good woman. Look after her, she looks after you. You saw her name, *Wahine*. In island language that means 'woman.' This is all the woman I have."

I grinned back at him.

"That makes two of us, Johnny."

He nodded and turned back to his stove, talking as he worked.

"Sometimes it is like that—there is one woman who is all woman, and when she is gone it is as if there were no women at all."

"You're a very wise man, Johnny," I said quietly.

I saw his dark shoulders lift in a shrug.

"We are the lost people, Renboss. But we are not all children or fools."

"Have you ever had a woman of your own, Johnny?"

He shook his head. "Where in this country would I find a woman of my own kind? Where, if I left this country, could I find the life which I have here? It is better this way, I think."

There was a small silence after that, while I smoked my cigarette and Johnny heated a can of stew and cut thick slices of bread which he buttered and laid on a tin plate.

When the meal was ready, he laid it on the cabin table and we sat down together. I felt again the curious sensation of separation and release which had come to me on the flight north. This man was my friend, my brother in adventure. The small, confined world between decks was the only real world, the rest was all illusion and fantasy.

When we had finished eating, we washed the plates and went up on deck. Sitting on the hatch cover, we saw the sun go down in a crimson glory, and then it seemed, at one leap, the stars were out, low-hung, in a purple sky. The wind was blowing inshore, and we heard the slap of the water as the *Wahine* rose and fell to the rhythm of the small waves.

Johnny Akimoto turned to me.

"Something you should understand, Renboss."

"What's that, Johnny?"

"This boat. She is mine, as if she were my woman. I understand her, she understands me. So long as we are on board, I must be the master. On the island it is the other way. It is your island—you say what is to be done, I will do it. We understand that, both of us."

"I understand it, Johnny."

"Then there is nothing more to be said between us."

"There is one thing, Johnny."

"What is that?"

"Before I came on board today, I telephoned a friend of mine in Sydney. If there's trouble, he'll come up and join us."

"This friend of yours—what sort of man is he?"

"He is an Italian, Johnny—a skindiver. He was a frogman with the Italian navy during the war."

"Sounds like a good one. He has promised to come?"

"Yes."

"It is always good to have friends at a time like this. Come below. I want to show you something."

We tossed our cigarettes into the water and went back to the cabin. Johnny Akimoto opened a cupboard under the bunk and took out two rifles. They were .303s, army pattern, but they were freshly oiled and the bolts slid home smoothly and true.

Johnny looked at me and grinned.

"I have had these a long time. I have never used them, except for rabbits and wallabies. If there is trouble, we shall not meet it unarmed."

"What about ammunition?"

"Two hundred rounds. It goes on your bill."

He put the rifles back in the cupboard and closed the door.

"Now I think we should sleep. We start at first light."

I peeled off my clothes and threw myself on the bunk, drawing a single sheet over me for covering. I heard Johnny go on deck to set the riding lights. I saw him come down and turn out the hanging lamp in the cabin. Then I slept and I did not dream at all.

We woke to fresh sunlight and a flat calm. I dived

overside for a freshener, while Johnny stood on the deck with the rifle in case of sharks. When I hauled myself aboard on the anchor cable, Johnny went over in his turn.

Then we started the diesel, hauled in the anchor and nosed the *Wahine* out, eastering first, then turning southward to the Whitsunday channel and the bright islands where the tourists come.

Johnny was at the wheel, standing straight and proud—proud of the boat which was his woman, proud of himself and his mastery of her. We ate in the sun, watching the coast slide green and gold past our starboard quarter and the small smudges ahead grow to green islands with the lacework of white water round them.

It was a three-hour run at cruising speed. Allowing another hour for loading, Johnny proposed that we should lunch before we left for our own Island of the Twin Horns. There was a matter of courtesy, he explained. The tourists were one thing. They came and paid their money and had their fun and went away, leaving little but a memory of laughter by day and whispers under the palms by night. But with the island people themselves it was a different thing. There was the drink to be taken together, the news to be exchanged, the small local news which they made themselves and in which the transient tourists had neither interest nor part. There were favours to be done: the repair of a generator, a fault in the refrigeration system, a note to be taken to a guesthouse on a neighbouring island. We must attend to our own business, to be sure, but we would not cut ourselves off from the concerns of the small family of which we were now a part.

I pleaded caution, remembering that one day, sooner or later, Manny Mannix would come flaring like a hunter for the traces of Renn Lundigan. To Johnny Akimoto my reason was unreason.

"These are good people," he said. "Make yourself one of them, they will be one with you when trouble comes. You never know how or when you may need them."

I had no choice but to agree with him. I asked myself what I should have done without this grave, strong islander, alien in blood but still no stranger, who stood at the wheel like some ancient god, his muscles rippling to the play of the wheel, his skin shining like silk in the sun.

We were halfway there when Johnny gave me the wheel while he went up to the forepeak and stood whistling like the old lugger captains for a wind.

We didn't need a wind. The diesel was throbbing smoothly and pushing us through the flat water at a steady eight knots. But Johnny wanted a wind. Johnny wanted to hoist sail and show me how his woman performed, when the sweet wind filled the canvas and laid her over on her side. But the calm persisted and I was glad of it. There was no work at the wheel, and I could surrender myself to the soft magic of sun and water and the silence of men who understand each other and have no need for words.

It was eleven in the morning when we made our landfall—a small island of coral with a long, low building in the center and small white huts dotted among the palms. The coral beach dropped sharply into six fathoms of water and we cut the motors and let the *Wahine* drift in to close anchorage.

The tourists came down in a body to meet us—brown girls in bright bathing suits, brown boys with their arms round the shoulders of the girls, the island staff in print frocks or khaki shorts, following behind like shepherds of the holiday flock.

Some of the bathers swam out to us and tried to clamber up the anchor cable, but Johnny Akimoto refused to allow them on deck. His ship was his own and none might come aboard except as his guest. We dropped into the dinghy and rode the few yards to the beach, where Johnny returned the familiar greetings with grave courtesy and introduced me as his friend, Mr. Lundigan, who had bought a place nearby and had come to pick up his stores. The island folk gave me a warm greeting but asked few questions, content to accept me at the value Johnny had given me.

They told me that my crates had arrived safely. I was able to relax again and enjoy the cold beer and the tropical salad and the easy hospitality of these dwellers on the inner reef.

When I told them the name of my island, they laughed. When I confounded them with news of a channel and a water supply, they nodded sagely and pointed the moral that the Government didn't know everything—even though it might pretend to. When I talked in cagey generalities about underwater exploration, they were frankly and embarrassingly interested. The island dwellers have a naïve and touching pride in the wonderland that surrounds them. Each has his tally of small discoveries or his small hoard of collector's pieces—cowries, quaint corals, bailer shells, flotsam and jetsam from forgotten wrecks.

Again they repeated the chemist's story of the girl student who had passed their way, making the short hops between the islands in an open skiff with a puttering outboard motor. I was sorry to tell them I had never met her. I was happy in the private thought that I never would.

Then, mercifully, the meal was over. We had no errands to run. We had only to hoist the crates on board the *Wahine*, up anchor and head north by east for the Island of the Twin Horns. I smiled my way through the small ceremonies of farewell, passed some banal backchat with the tourists who came down to cheer us off . . . and then we were free again, with a freshening breeze to gladden the heart of Johnny Akimoto and a bellying jib that gave us two knots better than the steady, chugging diesel.

Johnny nursed the *Wahine* onto the wind like a lover. He held her on the tack like a master. He stood at the wheel, strong legs straddled against the buck, head thrown back, eyes shining and white teeth grinning in triumph. He shouted to me, "She's a beauty, my *Wahine*, eh, Renboss?"

"She's a beauty, Johnny. What time do we raise the island?"

"Hour and a half. Two, maybe."

"Nice work, Johnny. That gives us daylight to unload and make camp."

He nodded, grinning still, and twitched the wheel a fraction, to follow the faint shift of the wind. Then he began to sing, a warm, crooning island song in the language of his mother's people. The words were a mystery to me, but the melody caught at my heart and I was glad for him and sad with him and very grateful that Johnny Akimoto had made me his friend.

It was three in the afternoon when we raised the island. I stood in the forepeak, braced against the stays, and watched it grow from a grey smudge to a green blur and then to a horned island with a crescent of beach. In a little while I could trace the contours of the rocks and distinguish the separate trunks of the great pisonia trees. There was the group of pandanus that marked the spring. There was the surfline on the outer reef and the shifting green of calm water inside the lagoon. I watched it grow and grow, filling our horizon, and I felt like a man coming home from the wars to his father's house.

I turned and shouted to Johnny, "You know the channel, Johnny?"

He raised a hand in acknowledgment and shouted back, "I know him, Renboss!"

"You going to take her in with the engine? It's fast and narrow."

He shook his head. His eyes were full of bright challenge.

"I sail her in, Renboss . . . I sail her."

And sail her he did. With every stitch of canvas she could carry. A hundred yards from the reef he brought her round on a short tack. He lined her up with the western horn and the single beach oak, and set at the reef like a horse to a hurdle. I felt her leap as she hit the first roller, then Johnny laid her hard over and drove her like a racer through the rip, while I watched openmouthed and waited for the coral trees to rake the bottom out of her and strip her to the keelson.

A minute later we were through, sliding with way on through glassy water, with the white beach in front and fear and uncertainty and Manny Mannix a thousand miles behind.

I shouted and cheered and danced the deck for sheer happiness, while Johnny nosed the *Wahine* into anchorage.

We dropped the hook and stowed the canvas and were just preparing to take the dinghy ashore on the first run when I saw something that killed my happiness with one stroke and set me cursing obscenely in a cold fury. . . .

At the head of the beach, where the trees began, a small tent had been pitched—and below it, careened above the tidemark, was a small skiff with an outboard motor.

Chapter Seven

"Easy, Renboss . . . take it easy now."

Johnny Akimoto was at my elbow, his warm voice chiding gently, talking me from madness to anger, from anger to common sense.

"It's only the girl, Renboss. You know—the one they told us about at the guesthouse."

"I know! I know!" I shouted the words at him. "The bloody little naturalist with her put-put and her collection of bloody sea slugs. Why the hell did she have to come here? Doesn't she know this is my island?"

"No, Renboss, she doesn't know that," said Johnny quietly.

"Then she damned soon will. Come on, Johnny, get the dinghy. I'll have her off the beach in twenty minutes."

"You can't do that, Renboss."

There was that in Johnny's voice which gave me pause. He laid his hand on my arm in a gesture of restraint.

"Why can't I? She doesn't have to stay here, does she?"

He pointed back to the reef and the channel we had just passed.

"You see? The tide is running in now. In the channel it makes five, six knots. With a boat like that, and a toy motor like that, how would she get through? And if she did, she could not reach the nearest island for three hours. By that time it is dark and dangerous."

I had no answer to that. I stared moodily across the water to the beach and wondered vaguely why the girl didn't show up. She must have seen us coming.

Johnny spoke again. "Renboss?"

"Yes?"

"In a minute or two we go ashore. We meet this girl. We tell her who we are. We tell her that she must leave us soon as possible. But we do it gently."

"Why?"

"Because she is young. Because she will be a little afraid. Because it is easier to be kind to someone than hard. Because it would be bad to have her spread the story that you are an unpleasant man who does not understand the manners of the Reef. . . . And because we are both gentlemen, Renboss."

I looked up at him. His mild, wise eyes pleaded with me not to disappoint him. I gulped down my anger and gave him a crooked smile of apology.

"All right, Johnny. Be damned to you. We'll be kind to little bluestocking. But I tell you now, I'll have her off this island tomorrow or my name's not Renn Lundigan."

His face broke into a wide smile of approval. He clapped me on the shoulder and walked aft to haul in the dinghy for the first load of stores.

We were halfway to the beach when I gave voice to the thought that had been plaguing me for the last ten minutes.

"Funny thing, Johnny, the tent's there . . . the boat's beached. . . . Where's the girl?"

"Round the other side, perhaps, in the rock pools."

"She's a damn fool if she is, with the tide running in. There's a sheer wall round there. If she's not careful she'll be spending the night on a ledge."

"Maybe she's sleeping."

"Maybe."

Johnny grinned at my ill humour and bent to the oars again. Nothing more was said until we had beached the dinghy and were striding up towards the tent. The flaps were open and the guys were slack. A careless job. She'd be lucky if it didn't tumble about her ears at the first puff of the night wind. I hailed her.

"Hello, there! Anybody home?"

My voice was flung back at me from the circling ridge, but there was no answer from the tent. I was two strides ahead of Johnny when we reached it, so I was the first to see her.

At first glance I thought she was dead. Her dark hair was lank and matted about her cheeks and temples. Her face was the colour of old ivory. Her cotton blouse was torn open, exposing her small round breasts. One hand trailed limply on the sandy floor, the other lay slackly across her belly. She wore a pair of faded denim shorts. One leg was outflung on the stretcher. The other dangled over the side. It was swollen and blue from knee to instep.

Then I saw that she was alive. Her breathing was shallow, laboured. I felt her pulse. It was thready and flickering. There were beads and runnels of perspiration on her face and neck and breast. She looked like a limp rag doll left by little girls at playtime.

I looked up at Johnny Akimoto. He said nothing, but bent and examined the swollen limb. He flexed the ankle joint so that the sole of the foot tilted upwards. The girl stirred in a sudden spasm of pain but did not awaken. Johnny motioned to me to look. Then he traced with his finger the small lines of punctures stretching from the ball of the toes to the ridge of the heel. Seven of them. He shook his head gravely and said one word, "Stone-fish."

The stonefish is the ugliest fish in the world. Its grey-brown body is a mass of wart-like growths. It is coated with thick foul slime. Its mouth is a gaping semicircle, opening upwards and livid green inside. Along the ridge of its spine are thirteen needle-sharp quills, each with its own poison sac. Its sting can kill a man or cripple him with racking agonies for weeks. There is no known antidote to its poison. The natives of the north dance the stonefish dance in their initiation ceremonies so that young bucks may know the danger that lies in wait in the crevices of the coral reefs.

I questioned Johnny Akimoto.

"Will she die, Johnny?"

"I don't think so, Renboss. She is very sick. She has fever, as you see. She sleeps because she is worn out with that and the pain. But she will not die, I think, unless the poison in the leg gets worse."

"We shall have to get her to a doctor, Johnny."

Johnny shrugged. "I have seen what the doctors do with this sort of thing. They know as little as we do about the poison of the stonefish."

"But, damn it all, Johnny, she can't stay here! We can't look after her."

"Why not? We have the medicine chest. We have sulfa and the other drugs. We know what to do. Besides, if we take her to the mainland, we lose two days. A day there . . . a day back."

A wise fellow, Johnny. A shrewd, secret man from the old islands. He knew better than I did, myself, what would bend me to his wishes. I resigned myself to the situation.

"All right, Johnny, have it your way. Get back to the *Wahine* and bring the medicine chest—and a couple of clean sheets while you're about it."

"Yes, Renboss," said Johnny.

He gave me a small ironic smile and walked swiftly out of the tent.

When he had gone, I settled the girl more comfortably
on the stretcher and looked around. There was a small
folding table loaded with stoppered jars of marine
specimens. There were bottles of acetone and formal-
dehyde. There were scalpels and tweezers and scissors
and a good microscope. There was a canvas chair and a
bucket and a collapsible canvas basin. There was a
rucksack with clothes and towels and a small cosmetic
case. On the face of it, the girl was a genuine student
who knew her job and worked at it.

Against this was the fact that she had walked the reef
in bare feet . . . an intolerable folly that had nearly
killed her and might well wreck my plans for the raising
of the treasure ship.

I settled her more comfortably on the narrow stretcher, then took the bucket and walked up to the spring
under the pandanus tree. Had I come to the island as I
had hoped to come, I might have gone running and
singing. Now I was full of the flat taste of disappointment. I filled the bucket with fresh, cool water, and as I
walked back I saw Johnny Akimoto casting off the loaded
dinghy for the pull back to shore.

He waved to me and I waved back, but in spite of the
comradely gesture I was irritated with Johnny Akimoto.
All very well for him to be bland and logical about the
situation. This was my island, as the *Wahine* was his
boat. This was . . . Then I saw the humour of it, saw
what a cross-grained creature disappointed greed can
make of a frustrated don. I began to chuckle, and by the
time I reached the tent I was in reasonable humour
again.

I poured water into the canvas basin. I rummaged in
the rucksack for clean clothing. I found a fresh towel and
a washcloth. Then, turning back to the girl on the bed, I
began to bathe her. I stripped off the dank clothing and
sponged the fever sweat from her body.

She groaned and opened her eyes as the cold water flowed over her. But her expression was blank and she mumbled unintelligibly, then fell limply back against the sodden pillow.

Sickness is never beautiful. The service of a sick body provokes pity but not desire. The girl, cradled in my arms, was beautiful, there was no doubt of that; but fever and shock and the wrenching pains of the poison had marred her beauty and left her like a wax image, without pulse or passion, almost without life.

I had just finished dressing her in the fresh clothes when Johnny Akimoto came back. He nodded approval, then set the medicine chest on the table and took out the scalpel, which he sterilized carefully in the flame of a cigarette lighter. There was a delicacy and precision about his movements that made me wonder what education and opportunity might have done for this calm, deep man, whose alien blood had condemned him to isolation among his white brothers.

"Let her lie back," said Johnny. "I want you to help me."

We knelt at the foot of the stretcher and I took the girl's foot in my hands, tilting it and holding it firm, while Johnny made a deep incision along the line of the spine marks. The girl groaned and writhed, while a great gush of fetid matter spurted from the puffy flesh. Johnny drained the wound, washed it, dressed it generously with sulfa powder and bound it with clean gauze. I watched, gaping, while he took a syringe and injected a careful measure of penicillin into the girl's arm.

"Where did you learn this, Johnny?" I could not keep the surprise from my voice.

"In the army, Renboss," said Johnny calmly. "I was a medical orderly at Salamaua field hospital."

He took the ampule out of the syringe and laid it carefully back in its container.

"We sterilize these things later, when we have hot water."

I agreed meekly. "Yes, Johnny."

The girl was moaning now, fighting her slow way back to consciousness. I lifted her and held her in my arms while Johnny stripped the stretcher and remade it with one of our palliasses and a pair of clean sheets. Then we laid her down again, drew the sheet over her and watched a little till the moaning subsided and she slept again, breathing more regularly and deeply. Then we left her. We had work of our own to do.

We pitched our tent in an angle of rocks a few paces from the spring. It was out of the wind and sheltered from the heat by the spreading green of an ancient pisonia. We dug a drain round it to carry off water if the rain should come. We built an oven of stones against a rock wall. We unrolled sleeping bags on the framed stretchers and disposed our few personal belongings out of the reach of ants and spiders.

We filled our big canvas water bag and hung it, dripping, on the tent pole to cool. We slung a tarpaulin between four tree trunks and stacked our crates of equipment underneath it, draining the ground round them as we had drained the tent. Only fools like to rough it. The secret of a working camp is to keep it tidy, clean and dry.

Now at last we were at home. Johnny Akimoto lit a fire while I brought a billy of water from the spring and set it on to boil. We lit cigarettes and sat down to smoke while the dry wood sputtered and crackled and the small flames rose round the blackened sides of the billy.

It was a placid moment, a good moment. Had it not been for the girl in the tent on the beachhead, it would have been a perfect moment. I turned to Johnny Akimoto.

"Now, Johnny, suppose you tell me."

"About what, Renboss?"

"About tomorrow, Johnny."

"Tomorrow?" said Johnny calmly. "Tomorrow we start work."

"But the girl, Johnny. What about the girl?"

"The girl is ill, Renboss. She will not be able to move for days yet."

"But she'll be able to talk, won't she, Johnny? She'll be curious, won't she, Johnny? All women are, Johnny. What do we tell her when she asks questions?"

"We tell her the truth, Renboss. We tell her that you are learning to be a skindiver and to use the apparatus for breathing under water. That is what you will be doing, isn't it?"

"Yes, I suppose it is. But I'll be doing more than just training."

Johnny flicked the butt of his cigarette into the flames.

"If you are wise, Renboss, you will do nothing more than that. You will find from the first moment that you put on the mask and make your dive into deep water that you are like a child learning his first steps. You will be uncertain. You will be afraid. You will be surrounded by monsters. You will have to live and move among them like one of themselves. You will have to learn which of them are enemies to be feared. You will have to learn to manage your own body in the simplest exercises of going down and coming up and moving yourself from one place to another. I tell you now, so that none of the time you give to this will be wasted. You will need all your courage and all your skill when you come to dive for the treasure ship."

Try as I might I could not shake the logic of this calm-voiced islander. I might defy it; but that could mean my own destruction and the end of all my hopes. I shrugged in wry resignation.

"All right, Johnny. We practice, we practice for days—

a week, maybe. By then the girl's moving around. She's bored. She wants company. She's curious about what is going on. She's a scientist, remember, Johnny. She won't buy the fairy tales we sold the others."

"Then," said Johnny simply, "I load her stores on the *Wahine*, take the boat in tow and deliver her to the mainland."

I was beaten and I knew it, but I was irritable and refused to let the matter drop so easily.

"She's ill, Johnny. We've still got to feed her and nurse her."

"We have to feed ourselves, too, so that is nothing. As for the nursing, it is a matter of changing the dressing, morning and night. Medicine she can take herself. We make her comfortable, then leave her till mealtime."

The water was bubbling in the billy. I heaved myself up to make the tea, but Johnny Akimoto laid a hand on my shoulder and drew me down again. His eyes were steady. His voice was firm.

"Renboss, there is something that must be said. I will say it and then perhaps you will tell me to take my boat and the girl and leave the island. If not, then I will stay and we will never mention it again between us. I know what you want to do. I know how much and why you want to do it. It is a good thing for a man to want something at the limit of his strength. It can also be a very bad thing. When I was diving for the pearling masters, there were those we hated and feared. They would go out to a new bed in the deep waters. They would find good pearls—enough to pay the divers and the crew and the expenses of the boat, and still leave a fine profit for the master, but they would not be satisfied. They would send the boys down again and again, deeper and deeper, until their eardrums burst and blood spurted out of their mouths and nostrils, and the bends knotted them up so that they could never work again. It is a bad thing, Renboss, when a man is so hungry for money that he can spare neither thought nor pity for anyone else in the world. . . . Now it is said. If you want, I will leave in the morning."

The billy boiled over. The steam rose in hissing clouds from the blackened coals at the edge of the fire, but neither of us moved. I tried to speak, but the words were slow in coming. Shame stifled them in my throat. Johnny Akimoto sat silent, a gentle man waiting without regret for me to accept or reject him.

Then mercifully the words came. I turned to him and held out my hand.

"I'm sorry, Johnny. I'd like you to stay."

He took my hand, his dark face split into a smile of sheer delight.

"I stay, Renboss. Better we make tea now. The girl will be awake soon and she will be hungry."

Together we prepared a simple meal, and when it was ready we carried it together down to the girl's tent.

She was feverish again. Her face was flushed. She was soaked with sweat and she tossed and moaned and plucked at the sheet as her temperature rose and the pains racked her. She shivered violently and drew the sheet up to her neck for warmth.

I sponged her again and held her up while Johnny forced water and a couple of tablets between her chattering teeth. Then we laid her back on the pillow and made our own meal, while the shadows lengthened outside and the first stirring of the night wind raised small eddies in the sand.

"She is worse than I thought," said Johnny. "If the fever does not break tonight . . ."

He left the rest of it unsaid.

"One of us should stay with her tonight, Johnny."

He nodded. He was pleased that I had said it.

"We should take her up to our tent, Renboss. She can

use my stretcher. Then, maybe, you can get some sleep.
If she needs you, you are there."

I looked at him, curiously. I could not read what was in
his mind. I questioned him.

"But what about you, Johnny? There's no need to
move out. We can both—"

"No, Renboss. I will sleep down here."

"I don't see what you're driving at."

Johnny smiled with gentle irony.

"She is young, Renboss," he said. "She is young and
sick and lonely. If she woke tonight and saw a black man
bending over her, then she would be afraid."

Johnny Akimoto's father was a Japanese exile. His
mother was a dark woman from the Gilbert Islands.
Johnny himself was one of the lost people who would live
without love and die without a son to succeed him. But
of all the men I have ever met, Johnny Akimoto was
most a man.

We wrapped the girl in the sheets and carried her up
to the big tent. Leaving Johnny to settle her, I walked
back to pick up the medicine chest. As I bent to pick it
up, I noticed a small leather wallet wedged between two
bottles on the folding table. I opened it.

There were a few bank notes, some postage stamps
and a letter of credit from the Commercial Banking
Company. It was endorsed "Miss Patricia Mitchell."
Now at least we knew her name and the fact that she was
single. I folded the paper and put it back in the wallet.
The rest she could tell us herself when she recovered—if
she recovered.

Johnny seemed to have his doubts about that and I
didn't care to dwell on what might happen if she died
while she was in our hands: police inquiries, a coroner's
inquest, stories in the newspapers, gossip along the
coast. The secret of the *Doña Lucia* and the gold of the
King of Spain would be a secret no longer.

The sun was going down when I left the tent: a golden ball rolling off the edge of the world into a sea of yellow and crimson, ochre and royal purple. I stood and watched it disappear behind the rim of creation. I saw the brief glory of the afterglow. I watched the colours fade from the surface of the ocean and the peach bloom brushed from the sky by the swift fingers of the night. Then I turned slowly and walked up to the tent.

The girl was still in the grip of fever and Johnny Akimoto was waiting to bid me good night.

Chapter Eight

I stripped down to a pair of shorts and stretched out on the camp bed. But I could not sleep. My nerves were tight as piano wires, and I could not shut my mind to the mumblings of the sick girl on the other side of the tent or to the steady beat of the sea and the small creaking of restless birds in the flame tree outside.

I got up, lit the kerosine lamp, fished in my bag for the notes Nino Ferrari had given me and began to study them. They were simple, dry, precise; an elementary exposition of the principles of free diving with a static air supply. They spoke of the relation of pressure to depth; of the accumulation of free nitrogen in the bloodstream; of the dynamics of motion in deep water; temperature variations and symptoms of narcosis; and positive control of the Eustachian tubes.

I read them, line by line, but they made no impression on me. I was a man beset with visions. Visions of coral gardens, and monstrous fish in rainbow colours, and a shadowy ship festooned with sea grasses in whose holds lay chests of gold guarded by antique horrors.

I heard the girl chattering and moaning as the fever shook her again. I got up and held the lamp high to look at her. I was shocked and frightened. Her lips were blue. There were great shadows round her sunken eyes, which stared blindly at the yellow light. I put the lamp down while I bathed her face and neck and hands. I forced two tablets between her lips and washed them down with water, which splashed on the covers as I held the glass to her chattering mouth. Then I settled her back against the pillow and, pulling a packing case to the foot of the stretcher, I sat down to wait.

It was three in the morning when the fever broke. Great spasms racked and twisted her and her moaning rose to a high bubbling sound. Then suddenly she seemed to collapse. A foul sweat broke out over her body and ran down her cheeks into the hollows of her neck and breast. She seemed to struggle for air and then lay very still. I felt her pulse; it was weak but steady. Her breathing became regular again; and, when I held a glass of water to her lips, she opened her eyes and said firmly, "I don't know you."

I grinned at her and said, "You soon will. I'm Renn Lundigan. You're Pat Mitchell. I saw the name in your wallet."

That puzzled her. She closed her eyes and turned her head slowly from side to side on the pillow. When she looked at me again, I could see she was afraid.

"I've been sick, haven't I?"

"Very sick. You stepped on a stonefish. You're lucky to be alive."

Memory was stirring slowly now. She struggled to sit up. I pressed her gently back onto the pillows.

"Just lie there. There's plenty of time. It'll come back if you take it easy."

She sighed fretfully like a child.

"I don't remember this place. Where am I?"

"You're on my island. This is my tent."

"Did you bring me here?"

"To the tent—yes. To the island—no. You were here when I came. You needed looking after, so we brought you up here for the night."

"Who's—we?"

"Johnny Akimoto and myself. Johnny's a friend of mine."

"Oh."

Suddenly she seemed to droop. The worn body was refusing its functions. She closed her eyes, so that I thought she had fallen asleep. Then she opened them again.

"Please . . . could I have a drink? I'm thirsty."

I held the glass to her lips, raising her head while she drank greedily, choking on the last mouthful. Then I lowered her to the pillow and she thanked me gravely, like a small schoolgirl.

"That was nice. Thank you very much."

I turned away to get rid of the glass of water and then, when I looked at her again, she was asleep.

I drew the covers over her and closed the flap of the tent to keep out the wind. I threw myself on the stretcher, bone-weary, but no longer depressed. It was as if we had fought a battle together and won it. In a few minutes I, too, was asleep.

Johnny Akimoto brought us our breakfast: coral trout, fresh caught and grilled on the coals, thick buttered bread, tea sweetened with condensed milk. He grinned broadly when he saw the girl awake and with an anxious, puzzled smile on her worn face. I made the introductions.

"Pat Mitchell, this is Johnny Akimoto, my good friend. Johnny, this is Pat."

"I should thank you both. I . . . I don't seem to remember very much."

"We were worried about you, Miss Pat," said Johnny. "This morning I thought you might be dead. I looked in and saw you both sleeping. I thought maybe you would like fresh fish for breakfast."

He laid the tin plate on the side of the bed and

watched anxiously while she propped herself on one elbow and began to pick at it.

"You like it, Miss Pat? He was a big fellow. All of four pounds."

His eyes lit up when she smiled at him and said quietly, "It's very nice, thank you, Johnny."

We ate together—talking little. The fish was sweet eating, and the new sun warmed us through the grey canvas of the tent. I saw the colour flow slowly back into the girl's face as she nibbled at the food and drank mouthfuls of the steaming tea.

She raised her head and looked at me. The question seemed to worry her. She took time to phrase it.

"It was a stonefish, you said?"

"That's right. Don't you remember?"

"Not very well. I was walking on the reef . . ."

"Silly to walk on the reef barefoot."

She was instantly angry.

"I wasn't barefoot. I know better than that. I was wearing sandshoes. There was a pebble in one of them. I stopped to take it out. I overbalanced and slipped into a pool. My bare foot must have landed on the stonefish."

Johnny and I grinned at her small, weak anger. She flushed and went on.

"I don't remember how I got back. The pain was frightening. I seemed to be paralyzed. I fell several times. I remember wondering if I'd be caught by the tide. After that . . . nothing. How long have I been sick?"

"We don't know. We only arrived last night. You were unconscious when we found you."

A sudden thought came to her. Cautiously she drew back the sheet and looked at her bandaged leg.

"You dressed this for me?"

"Johnny did. He had to open it. You won't be able to walk for a while."

"No . . . I suppose not." Again the cautious framing

of the question. "These . . . these aren't the clothes I was wearing on the reef."

I turned away and fumbled for a cigarette, but Johnny Akimoto answered her with never a smile.

"You were very sick, Miss Pat. Renboss had to change your clothes and wash you."

She blushed ripe red; then her chin went up bravely and she said, "You've been kind and gentle to me. I'm very grateful."

"More tea, Miss Pat?" said Johnny, the courtly gentleman.

"Thank you, Johnny. I seem to be dried out."

Johnny took the tin mug and went out to the fire to fill it again. She turned to me.

"You told me last night this was your island."

"That's right."

"I didn't know that. I didn't mean to trespass."

"You weren't trespassing." I stumbled over it, lamely. "When you're well again, Johnny can take you back to the mainland."

"There's no need for that. I've got my own boat. I don't want to give you any more trouble."

It was an awkward moment. Courtesy might betray me into the very situation I wanted to avoid. The girl had been ill. She was handling an embarrassing interlude with some charm and more dignity than I myself could muster. But the fact remained: I wanted her off the island as quickly as possible.

Then Johnny came back with the tea and a suggestion that gave me time to think.

"You have been sick, Miss Pat. You are still sick, although the fever is gone. You must rest as much as you can. If you like, we will carry you down to the beach. We can make a shade for you with the tent fly, and you can watch us while we work."

Her face brightened. "I'd like that. I could sleep. I

could write up some notes. And as you say, I could watch you work. What sort of work is it?"

"Renboss, here, wants to learn skindiving. I have come out to teach him."

She laughed at that, strongly, happily.

"That's not work. That's play."

"The way Johnny teaches, it's hard work. You wait and see."

My bluff adventurer's manner didn't deceive her for a moment. She gave me a long, level look and said quickly, "This is your island, Mr. Lundigan. Whatever you choose to do here is your own affair. I promise you I'll mind my business and leave you as soon as I can travel."

Johnny Akimoto choked convulsively, spluttered something about a fishbone and rushed from the tent. Miss Patricia Mitchell gave me a sidelong smile and settled back on her pillow.

"Renn Lundigan, eh? You were quite a legend in your day. I never thought I'd meet you face to face."

"I don't know what the devil you're talking about—"

"That's natural enough. They sacked you, didn't they? Dead drunk under the dean's window at nine in the morning."

I gaped at her, speechless. The smile died on her lips, and she laid a small, clammy hand on my own.

"I'm teasing you and it's not kind—after all you've done for me. I'm from Sydney, too, you see. I'm a reader in natural history at the university. Small world, isn't it?"

A small world, indeed. Too damned small, when a man's past follows him out to the last island on the last reef before the wide ocean. Anger boiled in me swiftly and spilled out in a spate of bitter words.

"All right . . . so you know me. But I don't want to know you. I don't want you here, but you're ill and I can't do anything about it. Understand this: so long as you're here, we'll care for you. We'll feed you, nurse you and make you as comfortable as may be. But as soon as

you can walk I want you gone. If you can't handle your
own craft, Johnny will take you back. Until then, don't
talk to me about the past. It's dead—done—finished.
Don't talk to me about friends. I have none. And when
you go, leave me in peace. Forget you've ever seen me."

I turned on my heel and walked out of the tent. I
thought I heard her weeping, but I didn't turn back. She
was the past and I wanted no part of her. The past was
dead and best forgotten. It was an illusion, of course. A
wild, crazy illusion. But I was still fool enough to cherish
it.

Johnny Akimoto rowed me out to a rock pool on the
inner fringe of the reef. He pulled easily across the oily
water, and when I looked back I could see the small
shelter on the sand where Pat Mitchell lay on her
stretcher looking out to sea. It was Johnny who had set it
up for her, Johnny who had carried her down and made
her comfortable and set the water bag within reach, and
dressed her wound and left the tablets at her hand.

Johnny. . . . Always Johnny. . . . Johnny's was the
strength and mine the weakness. Johnny's the calm
wisdom and mine the folly of frustration and flight. He
was sober and subdued as we rowed out, and if there was
pity in his eyes, I could not read it.

We moored the skiff to a niggerhead, one of those
jutting stumps of dead coral which are found all over the
reefs, and which have the look of a frizzled skull on top of
a stumpy neck. I took off my sandshoes and put on the
pair of flippers that Nino Ferrari had given me. They
were not the orthodox model with half sole and a heel
strap. They were made with a full sole and a heel grip so
that the diver might walk on the coral floor without too
much danger from stonefish and spiny urchins.

I buckled on the wide canvas belt, weighted with
seven pounds of lead slugs, with the long knife of
tempered steel in a sheath of plaited leather. Now I was
ready for the lung pack.

The two cylinders of compressed air were fixed to a frame of light alloy, and they fitted on my back as a knapsack fits on the back of a climber, with an arrangement of canvas braces slung on the shoulders and buckled under the breast. Two tubes of corrugated rubber, coated with cotton webbing, led from the cylinders to the polished metal disc of the regulator, which is the mainspring of the mechanical lung. Another tube of the same material terminated in a small rubber mouthpiece with slotted rubber lugs to be gripped between the teeth of the diver.

I set the regulator and Johnny Akimoto lifted the pack onto my back, settling the spine pad comfortably, while the straps were buckled and tested.

Now I was ready for the mask. I dipped it in the sea to wet the rubber and wash the Perspex so that it would not mist over under water. Then I slipped it over my head, moulded the rubber into my cheekbones and tried a breath to test whether it was watertight. Then I adjusted the strap at the back of my skull and slipped the mask up on my forehead.

Johnny Akimoto watched me with careful interest.

"Ready now, Renboss?"

"Ready, Johnny."

"Take a look first before you go down."

I sat down in the thwarts and looked over into the clear water. Coral pools vary in depth from a few inches to fifteen or twenty feet. This one was perhaps a dozen yards long and fifteen feet wide. Its depth was no more than two fathoms. Yet, like all the others on the reef, it was a perfect microcosm of the colourful and abundant life of the coral sea.

Soft sea grasses, green and red and gold, moved gently as if to an underwater wind. Purple-lavender corals spread like flowers in a summer garden. Red and white anemones spread their tentacles like the petals of a Japanese chrysanthemum. Soft corals in rainbow colours

lay like primitive frescoes on the rocky walls. Shoals of
small fish, striped and dappled, darted about among the
foliage. A blue starfish lay motionless on the sandy
bottom, and a hermit crab made a tentative foray from
the speckled cone shell which was his home. It was a
world of riotous colour and teeming life, and I felt a
sudden thrill at the thought that I was soon to be made
free in it. I looked up at Johnny.

"Ready, Johnny."

He grinned and nodded. I slipped the mask over my
eyes and nostrils, moulded it once more to my skin,
clamped the mouthpiece between my teeth, tested the
airflow and lowered myself over the stern into the pool.
The weighted belt took me down instantly. I sank to a
depth of four or five feet and hung suspended in a liquid
world.

My first sensation was one of utter panic.

I was surrounded by monsters. Magnified by the mask
and the water, the waving grasses were primeval forests.
The anemones were gaping mouths. The corals were
trees in an antediluvian forest. The shoals of fish were
armies from another planet. The hermit crab was a huge
and horrible deformity. I gasped and gagged and spat out
the mask and kicked myself to the surface to find Johnny
Akimoto leaning over the gunwale laughing at me.

He gave me his hand and pulled me up until I got a
grip on the timber, and I hung there, gasping and
spluttering.

"What happened, Renboss?" said Johnny Akimoto, his
white teeth flashing in a broad grin.

"I got scared. That's what happened. Everything's
different when you get down there."

Johnny nodded. "It is always like that, Renboss, the
first time. Now look again."

I looked down into the pool. There were no monsters.
It was the same narrow world of rare Lilliputian beauty
that I had seen the first time.

"Go down again, Renboss," said Johnny. "Take it easy this time. Breathe slow and even. Swim a little. Dive to the bottom. Take a good look at the things that frightened you the first time."

I nodded agreement, slipped the mask back over my face, clamped on the mouthpiece and let myself slide back into the pool.

For a long minute I hung suspended below the surface, forcing myself to concentrate on the simple involuntary act of breathing. After a while the rhythm returned to me. The air flowed freely from the cylinders. The bubbles from the regulator rose to the surface in a steady stream, with a soft palpitating hiss that matched the rhythm of my breathing.

My courage returned to me. I kicked gently with the flippers and found myself floating easily towards the coral wall.

Then I stopped short. A new terror confronted me. Naked hands, big as the branches of a tree, reached out to grasp me. From a shadowy recess between waving sea grasses a great mouth gaped to devour me and a pair of eyes as big as oysters surveyed me with calm malevolence. For a moment I was petrified. I wanted to do as I had done before, spit out the gag and kick myself to the surface. Then reason returned and self-control with it. The hands were staghorn corals. The eyes and mouth belonged to a small coral trout, which turned and flickered away with a flash of princely scarlet when I reached out my hand to touch it.

I kicked more strongly now. I found myself moving with a fabulous ease. The corals and the grasses slid past me with surprising speed. The labour of breathing at increased pressure was no longer apparent. I was seized with the illusion that I was a bird suspended between earth and heaven, that my arms were spreading wings and that the element surrounding me was air instead of water. I emptied my lungs and saw the air bubbles stream upwards as I dived downwards in a steep trajectory. There was a sudden pressure in my ears, a sharp pain in the sinus cavities. I swallowed as one does in a landing aircraft. The tubes cleared themselves and the pressure and the pain were gone. My hands clutched the sandy bottom.

With a series of movements that made me think, irrelevantly, of an acrobat on the high trapeze, I stood upright. There was no weight in my body, no hint of labour in the liquid motions of my limbs. When I walked it was as if I floated. When I floated it was as if I walked. Happiness took hold of me. A great goodwill pervaded me. I walked to the coral walls and swam along feeling the sea grass brush my face, reaching out to touch the branches, gingerly at first, then with more confidence, as if they were trees on my own land. I touched the anemones with my finger and saw the bright tentacles withdraw in fright. I hung motionless while the striped fish swam round my body and flashed away in terror at the slightest movement.

I don't know how long I stayed there, tasting the pleasures of my new citizenship in a new world. Then suddenly I was cold. I looked down at my body. It was covered with goose pimples. The skin of my fingers was white and crapy. It was time to go. With a flurry of hands and flippers I shot to the surface and hauled myself into the dinghy. Johnny told me I had been underwater for twenty-five minutes.

I shed my gear and sat quietly for a while, feeling the warmth flow out again from the core of my body to meet the warmth of the sun on my naked skin.

Johnny questioned me intently. "You did not find it hard this time, Renboss?"

"Not hard at all, Johnny. Once the first fear left me it was easy—child's play."

"The first part is always easy," said Johnny soberly. "The pool is shallow and enclosed. There is no work to do. There is no danger to think of, so you enjoy yourself. But this"—he reached forward and ran his finger along the seams of my shrunken hands—"this is the first danger—cold. You think you are not working, because you move easily. But your body is working all the time. It burns itself up to keep you warm. And when you go into deep water it is colder still . . . suddenly cold, as if you had crossed a fence from summer into winter. That is why a man cannot stay down too long in deep water. For a naked diver like me it is not so bad. I stay down only for a short while, so long as my lungs can hold the last mouthfuls of air, but you breathe down there and the cold creeps on you, makes you tired without your knowing it."

I nodded, remembering that Nino Ferrari had told me the same thing in other words, remembering his advice to wear a woolen jerkin for underwater work.

"We should go in now," said Johnny. "For the first time you have done enough. This afternoon we will try again. When you are not diving, you should eat well and exercise yourself. When we come to work, you will find that your strength spends itself quickly."

We unhitched the dinghy from the niggerhead and pushed off. The tide was running out fast now, and in an hour the lagoon would be a naked stretch of sand and the reefs would be exposed, dead and ugly in the sun, save where the pools remained guardians of the multitude of lives which spawn in its coral reaches.

As Johnny sculled steadily back to the shore, my eyes were fixed on the beach where Pat Mitchell lay under the canvas awning. I asked myself what I was going to say to her. I wondered what words would bridge the gap that I myself had cut between us. My decision was unchanged. I wanted her gone. But we would be together for days yet; and a tropic island may be a paradise, but it may also be a hell, if the people on it cannot live in harmony.

Johnny Akimoto sent the dinghy forward with one long powerful stroke; then he shipped his oars and spoke to me. "Miss Pat is sorry for what she said, Renboss. She wants to tell you, but she does not know how."

"Neither do I, Johnny, that's the trouble."

Johnny smiled gently. "She is a good one, that; what she promises she will do. When the time comes, she will go and she will leave you in peace. She has told you that, and she has told me, too."

I grinned at him then. I couldn't argue with Johnny.

"All right, Johnny. I'll talk to her. You get something to eat and leave me alone with her. I'll find something to say, though God knows what."

He dipped his oars again without saying another word. And when we came to the beach there was peace between us.

Chapter Nine

The noon sun was blazing on the canvas canopy; so we carried Pat Mitchell up to the big tent in the shade of the trees. Leaving Johnny to settle her, I walked outside to change into dry clothes—and to prepare my opening gambit.

When I came back she was alone, propped up on the stretcher with a small vanity case in her hand. I looked at her and saw that she was beautiful. Her cheeks were no longer yellow with sickness but tinged with brown from the sun, and lit from within with the growing fire of health. Her hair was no longer lank and matted but brushed soft and shining, drawn away from the face so that you could see the fine bones of the cheek and the small proud lift of the firm chin. Her eyes were dark but veiled in shyness. Her hands were capable and controlled on the coverlet.

She was all woman, this one, small, rounded and perfect like those statuettes of golden girls out of antique times. The stretcher creaked as I sat down on the foot of it. I took out a cigarette and offered her one, but she refused with a gesture. I lit up, smoked for a few moments to steady myself, then started to speak.

"Miss Mitchell . . . Pat . . ."

"No, Mr. Lundigan, let me say it."

She bent forward and spoke earnestly, carefully, as if

she were afraid to forget the lines she had rehearsed, as if the lines once spoken should fail to convey their meaning.

"What I said to you this morning was unpardonable. It was unnecessary and cruel, and I don't know why I said it. Or rather I do. It was because . . . because you had seen me with my clothes off, and you hadn't any right and . . . well . . . that's it and I'm sorry and I'll go away whenever you want me to and nobody will ever know that I have been here . . . nobody."

Then she lay back on the pillows as if exhausted. She looked at me as if afraid of what I might say or do. I tried to smile, but it wasn't a very successful effort. The smile is a sign of confidence. I was far from confident. I said, "I'm sorry, too. This is the first time I have been back to this island since . . . since my wife and I were here together. I can't explain how I felt about it. It was like— like a homecoming. I couldn't bear the thought of anyone else . . ."

"Intruding?"

"Yes—I must say it—intruding. But it wasn't your fault—it was mine. You couldn't know, even, that the island was mine. You were ill. You . . . Oh, to hell with it! I was a bloody boor. I'm sorry. Now can we talk about something else?"

She was smiling now; the breach was healed. She asked me for a cigarette. I gave it to her, lit it, and our talk led us away from the old dangerous grounds.

I told her how I had heard about her on the mainland. I told her of the young chemist who had lost his heart to her. I told her how she had impressed the islanders—a solitary girl put-putting between the islands in a tiny workboat. She laughed at that.

"Impressed? They thought I was crazy."

"I think you are, too. That's no sort of a boat for deep waters."

She shrugged. "It's all right if you're careful and wait for the weather. I've been lucky most of the time."

"Most of the time?"

She nodded. "I had my worst moment when I came here. The wind was high and the sea was freshening. I wasn't particularly worried. I was so close inshore. Then I couldn't find a channel."

"What did you do?"

"Rode up and down the reef until I found it."

"Dangerous."

"Yes, very. There was nothing else to do. Even when I got into the tide rip it was like trying to ride a bucking horse, but we got through all right."

I looked at the small firm hands on the sheet. Her mouth was firm, too—firm and smiling. A girl with heart and courage. I found myself beginning to warm to her. I thought that could be dangerous, too. I asked her some more questions.

"You're a naturalist. That's an odd job for a woman, isn't it?"

Her chin went up at that.

"I don't see why. I like it. I'm good at it. It pays fairly well and leaves me free to do the things I like."

"Such as—this?"

"That's right."

"What are you working at now?"

"A doctor's thesis. The ecology of *Haliotis asinina*— muttonfish to you, Renn Lundigan."

She had popped me back in my box and closed the lid with a bang. I couldn't help but be amused. Then it was my turn to be questioned.

"What about you, Renn? What are you doing now?"

"Johnny told you. Learning to dive."

"For pleasure?"

"For pleasure. Anything against it?"

"No. It makes a fascinating holiday, but what are you

going to do afterwards, Renn? For a living. I mean. You can't beachcomb here all your life."

I needed notice for that question. This was no playtime girl to be put off with fatuous backchat. I shrugged and made my little rueful mouth and said, "Well, I can't teach anymore. No university would have me. But I'm not a bad historian, and there is enough material around this reef to make a book or two. You know"—I waved my hands in a vague all-embracing gesture—"you know, the early navigators, the blackbirders, the pearling days . . . none of it's ever been properly documented."

Her eyes brightened. She leant forward with eager professional interest.

"That's good, Renn. That's very good indeed. This is the Barbary Coast of Australia, you know. There's all sorts of material here—piracy, violence, romance . . . everything. If I could write, that's what I'd like to do. Look, I'll show you something."

She snapped open her vanity case, tilted the lid back, lifted out a small tray and took out a small round object which she laid in the palm of my hand. For a long moment I stared at it, not daring to raise my eyes.

It was an exact replica of the old Spanish coin which Jeannette and I had found on the reef. I felt the blood drain from my face. My lips were dry. My tongue was too big for my mouth. I closed my eyes and saw my dreams blown down like a house of cards. I opened them again. The coin stared up at me from my palm, a golden eye, unblinking.

I looked at Pat Mitchell and asked her softly, "Where did you get this?"

Her explanation was eager and guileless. "Here, Renn. On the reef. It was the second day. I was poking round in a rock pool when I saw what looked like a piece of dead coral, flat and round. I don't know why I picked it up, except perhaps that its shape was a little unusual.

When I did, I saw that there was metal underneath—
tarnished, of course, and overgrown. I brought it back to
the tent, cleaned it up and . . . that's the result."

"I see."

"But you don't seem to understand, Renn." She was
puzzled by my sudden change of manner. "You don't
seem to realize what that coin means. It confirms the
theories that the old Spanish navigators came down this
way and that some of them were wrecked on the reef
islands. You're a historian, Renn. Surely you see the
significance of it?"

I saw it all right. I couldn't fail to see it. I saw that this
girl would go back to the mainland and tell her little
story and flourish her antique coin until some bright
press man saw it and made a filler paragraph out of it,
and then the jig would be up. Every damned holiday-
maker on the coast would descend on my island in search
of buried treasure, unless . . .

I must have spoken the word aloud, because Pat
Mitchell laid her hand on mine and quizzed me with
anxious puzzlement.

"Unless what, Renn?"

I was caught between the devil and the deep. To fob
her off with a story would bring the world to my
doorstep. To tell her the truth would make her an
unwanted partner in my enterprise—an arbiter of my
fortunes and my destiny.

Involuntarily I closed my fingers on the coin. I felt the
edges of it biting into my palm. Then I thought of Johnny
Akimoto and what he had said to me. "She is a good one,
that; what she promises she will do." If I trusted Johnny,
I should trust Pat Mitchell also. My fingers relaxed. I
looked at her again. Her eyes were full of grave concern.

She was quietly, "Have I said something wrong,
Renn?"

I shook my head. "No, nothing wrong. I want to show
you something."

I walked over to my bed, pulled my bag from underneath it and took out the bracelet I had bought from the girl in Lennon's Hotel. Then I laid the coin in Pat Mitchell's hand.

"There's the mate to your gold piece."

Her eyes widened. She held the two pieces together, examining them closely. When she spoke again, her voice was a small breath of wonder.

"Is this yours, Renn?"

"Yes."

"Where did you get it?"

"My wife and I found it on the reef, years ago. Probably in the same place that you found yours."

"What—what does it mean?"

The words came out slowly and deliberately, like coins dropping into a pool.

"It means, my dear, that the treasure ship *Doña Lucia*, bound from Acapulco to the Philippines, was wrecked on this island in 1732. And Johnny Akimoto and I have come here to find it."

There was a long, long silence. The two coins lay unnoticed on the white sheet between us. Neither of us looked at them. We were looking at each other. Then Pat Mitchell spoke, quite calmly.

"Thank you for telling me, Renn. You did me a great honour. You have nothing to fear from me. When I am better I shall go away as I promised. I'll leave my coin with you. Nobody else will ever know."

I said nothing. On the face of it, what was there to be said? I felt tired and spent. My eyes ached. I buried my face in my hands and pressed the palms hard against the lids . . . in the old familiar gesture of the harassed student working by night light. Pat Mitchell reached out, took my hands away and tilted my face up towards her.

"Does it mean so much to you, Renn?"

"Everything, I think."

"The ship went down two hundred years ago, Renn. You may never find her."

"I know that."

"What then?"

"I don't care to think about it."

"One day," she said softly, "one day you may have to think about it. I hope for your sake you will not be too unhappy."

She lay back on the pillows and closed her eyes. She looked very small and very tired and very, very desirable.

I brushed her cheek with my fingertips and left her.

Johnny Akimoto was bending over the fire, stoking it with driftwood. He straightened when he saw me. His calm eyes were full of questions.

I told him bluntly. "She knows, Johnny."

He looked at me, wondering. "Knows what, Renboss?"

"Why we are here—about the treasure ship—everything."

"You told her?"

"I had to, Johnny. She found this on the reef." I spun the coin in the air, caught it and slapped it into his palm. He looked at it for a long time without speaking.

"I had to tell her, don't you see, Johnny? If I hadn't . . ." He looked up at me. His dusky face was beaming.

"I understand, Renboss. I understand very well."

"Did I do right, Johnny?"

"I think you did right, Renboss," said Johnny Akimoto. "Now there are three of us."

It was easier now that there were no secrets between us. Every morning Johnny and I carried Pat down to the beach and made her comfortable under the awning. She was growing stronger now, and the area of infection was receding down the calf towards the ankle. Soon she would be able to hobble about, but for the present she had no choice but to lie on the stretcher under the canvas and read or doze or write up her notebooks or watch the small bobbing shape of the dinghy, where Johnny and I were diving.

We were working the outer fringe of the reef now—the small narrow shelf where the anchor hit sand at ten fathoms. We had not yet begun our search for the *Doña Lucia*. I was still training, adapting body and brain to new conditions of depth and pressure. I was learning the art of decompression—staging slowly to the surface ten or fifteen feet at a time, resting after each ascent to prevent the accumulation of nitrogen in the blood-stream. At first I clung to the anchor cable, measuring my ascent as if on a notched stick. In the fantastic underwater world it seemed at first like a link with reality, and in my first contacts with the strangeness and terror of deep waters I clung to it desperately, while I struggled to regain my self-control.

I made new acquaintances, too. Acquaintances who might become enemies but who seemed content for the present at least to regard me as a curious phenomenon in their undisputed territory: the long, slim Spanish mackerel with his predatory saw-toothed mouth; the big groper, huge and bloated; the scarlet emperor; the big snapper whose flanks are striped with broad arrows; and now and again a cruising shark.

At first I was terrified. Then I learnt to lie still, suspended in the blue water, while the fish stared at me coldly and then whisked off when I blew out a stream of bubbles or clapped my hands in the fashion of a child.

Johnny said little until he saw me gain confidence and then he talked to me calmly, logically, about danger.

"There is always danger, Renboss. Never forget that. We do not know how a fish thinks, so we cannot tell what he will do. A dog—yes, a horse—yes. They belong to our world. They have lived with us for thousands of years. But a fish—who knows? One day a shark may come at you. You will have little warning. He will swim towards you. He will stop. He will circle. Then go away, perhaps. And the next second he will be coming at you like a bullet."

I grinned sourly. "What then, Johnny?"

He shrugged. "You are in the world of fishes. You must fight like a fish—by swimming, by twisting and turning away, by trying to frighten him."

"And if he won't be frightened?"

"You have a knife. You must try to strike him in the belly. There is no other way."

Always it was the same lesson—conquer fear by understanding. Conquer danger by courage and common sense. Naked in the underwater world a man has no other weapons.

Sometimes Johnny himself would come down with me. I would see him swimming about fifty feet above clad in nothing but a mask and a breechclout and a belt with a long knife in a leather sheath. I would lie on my back and watch him. I would see his dark body double up like a jackknife, then stiffen into a long, shearing dive that brought him down eight, nine fathoms in a matter of seconds. Then I would see how the pressure of the water squeezed his belly and his lungs and his rib cage until I thought the bones must crack under the enormous strain, but he would still swim with me a little and grin behind his goggles and raise his hand in a comical gesture before he slanted upwards into the sunlight.

I was proud of my newfound skill, but Johnny's was an older one and a greater one. I could breathe. I had air in bottles on my back to keep me comfortable for an hour or more, but Johnny had nothing but two lungfuls and his own strength and skill and calm courage. Then, when the lessons were over, we would row back to the beach, totting the small sums of my new knowledge. And when the shadows lengthened we would sit beside the fire and eat the meal Johnny had cooked, while Pat Mitchell lay on the mattress and added her small, wise voice to the quiet flow of our talk.

One evening in the warm darkness she gave voice to a thought that had vexed me for a long time.

"About your treasure ship, Renn . . ."

"What about it, Pat?"

"I've thought about it a lot these last days. It was wrecked outside the reef, wasn't it?"

I nodded. "I think so. I think it must have been. When I was away from the island I used to believe there might be a possibility that she had been flung onto the reef itself and broken up. The finding of my coin seemed to confirm that. Now that I'm here, I'm not so sure."

Then Johnny Akimoto spoke. "I think it was outside, Renboss. I am sure it was outside."

"What makes you so sure, Johnny?" asked Pat.

"I will tell you, Miss Pat. This Spaniard—she is a bigger ship than my *Wahine*, yes?"

"Much bigger, Johnny," I said. "Two hundred tons—three hundred, maybe."

"So . . . Now look at the *Wahine*. She is a small boat, yet she draws five feet of water. It takes a big sea to lift a boat like that and throw it into the middle of the reef. More likely I think that your Spaniard drove straight onto the outer reef, stuck there, perhaps, until the water and the wind hauled him off and he sank on the ledge."

"It reads all right, Johnny," I said, "but how do you explain the coins in the rock pool?"

"That's the point I was making, Renn." Pat's voice was eager and full of conviction. "It wasn't the ship. It was the men."

"The men?"

"Yes. Think of what happens in a wreck. They are out of control in uncharted waters. They know there is land, but they have no idea whether it is inhabited or not. It's the natural instinct of men in danger to cling to whatever possessions they have. The ship strikes. They know she must founder. The boats are useless on the reef. They jump and try to swim to the island. What would a man take with him when he jumped?"

Johnny Akimoto's voice came out of the darkness.

"I can tell you that, Miss Pat. His knife and his money belt."

And there it was. A neat hypothesis, certainly. A piece of logic that gave me new respect for this small brown girl with the proud chin and the dark, flashing eyes. But there were other things I wanted to know.

"If that's the way it happened, some of them must have reached the shore. I've been all over the island and I've never seen any traces of them."

"No, Renboss," said Johnny. "If the ship broke up on the night of the storm, none of them would have survived. The surf would have rolled them over the reef and torn them to pieces. After that there would be the blood and the sharks. You see?"

"Yes, Johnny. I see. I see something else, too. If your theory and Pat's are right, then we've an even-money chance of finding the *Doña Lucia* on the outer shelf."

"That is if she did not break up, but foundered immediately."

"That's the even-money chance."

For the moment nothing more was said. It was a working theory. We should have to test it. And to test it, Johnny Akimoto and I would have to dive over hundreds of yards of shelf outside the reef, ten fathoms down. Deeper, perhaps, because the shelf was narrow in places and the *Doña Lucia* could have slid and rolled down the sloping edge into the blue depths of the ocean. And if she did, I would have to go down alone, because the limit of Johnny's dive was ten fathoms higher than mine.

Johnny Akimoto stood up and began to pile more brushwood on the fire. I went into the tent and brought back a blanket for Pat's shoulders. When we were seated again she made a small announcement.

"I walked today."

"What?"

"I walked. It was painful at first, but after I'd hobbled about for a while it wasn't too bad."

Johnny's deep voice chided her. "You shouldn't have done that, Miss Pat. You can't afford to take chances."

"It wasn't a chance really, Johnny. The swelling's gone down—most of it, anyway. If I do a little each day, it won't hurt me. . . ."

I caught the odd note in her voice and looked towards her, but her eyes were in shadow and I saw only the defiant lift of her chin.

"So now you can send me home any time you like."

Chapter Ten

A twig exploded into a shower of sparks. New flames leapt up among the driftwood. The noddy terns in the giant pisonia tree chattered stridently and then fell silent. There was the distant boom of the surf, the steady whisper of the wind, the creak of branches and the small rustle of leaves and beach grasses.

Between the three people on the outer edge of the circle of firelight there was a long silence. Then Pat Mitchell spoke again. Her voice was steady and controlled.

"Will you take me back, Johnny?"

Johnny's voice answered her from the shadows.

"That's for Renboss to say, Miss Pat. I work for him. This is his island."

And there it was laid neatly in my lap. A decision that I had to make at a moment when I had neither wish nor need to make it. Abruptly and unreasonably I was angry. I said bluntly, "Do you want to go back?"

"No."

I stood up. I tossed my cigarette away irritably. I heard the words come tumbling out and did not recognize my own voice.

"Then, if you can walk, you can damn well work. You can cook the meals and keep the camp tidy. You can plot the reef where I want it plotted. You can stay in the boat while Johnny and I go down together. And for God Almighty's sake keep your mouth shut and don't get under our feet."

With which courtly little speech I left them and walked down to the beach with the uneasy conviction that I had made a fool of myself.

The moon was rising, a great cold disc in a purple sky. Its track lay across the water in a broad blade of rippling silver. The *Wahine* lay in the middle of it, riding at anchor with bare spars, like a ghost ship.

Far out on the rim of the reef I could see the white froth of the surfline. I could see the uneasy water with the channel cut through the coral. I knew, almost to a yard, the position of the rock pools where Pat Mitchell had found her coin and where Jeannette and I found ours.

Jeannette . . . I realized with a shock that I had not thought of her for a long time. When I tried to recall her face I could not. There was a new face there, engraven on the tablets of memory, a small, brown, lovely gypsy face, crowned with dark hair. I knew that I had just committed a singular folly. I knew that I could not recall it. I looked out again towards the dark water beyond the reef. I told myself that the time of preparation was over. Tomorrow we would begin work.

Tomorrow Johnny and I would plot a line on the outer edge of the reef and we would search it, step by step, on the sea floor for a ship that had died more than two centuries ago. And if we did not find it, I would have to summon my small courage and move out from the safety of the shelf into the blue pelagic deeps beyond.

I would go down into a continent of giants—among the manta rays which fly like great bats through the blue twilight, among the killer sharks and the giant gropers. I would go down to the fringe of madness, where the detritus of life from the upper levels filtered down to feed the other lives, nameless, primitive, in the ooze of the ocean floor.

I was suddenly cold and afraid.

Johnny Akimoto's footfalls in the sand made me start like an animal.

"Miss Pat says to thank you, Renboss."

"I'm a fool, Johnny . . . a bloody fool."

"No, Renboss," said Johnny quietly. "No man is a fool when he does what his heart tells him to do."

"It's not a question of my heart, Johnny. It's a question of . . . of time—and convenience. We start work tomorrow."

"Yes, Renboss."

I raised my arm and pointed, drawing a wide arc across the sector of the reef where the coins had been found.

"That's where it will be, Johnny. Thirty, forty yards to the right of the channel and from there to the big niggerhead."

"That's a lot of water, Renboss."

"That's why we start work tomorrow."

"Miss Pat says to use her boat, Renboss. It is bigger than our dinghy and easier to work in the outside water."

"She is a shrewd one, isn't she, Johnny?" I said, with sour admiration.

"No, Renboss, she is not shrewd. She wants to show us that she is grateful for letting her stay."

I shrugged. "Perhaps, but she knows what she wants, doesn't she?"

"Yes, Renboss. She knows what she wants."

"And what does she want, Johnny?"

"Why not ask her yourself? Good night, Renboss."

He gave me a wide grin, turned on his heel and left me.

I walked slowly up the beach to the big tent. I brushed my teeth and sluiced my face from the water bucket. I doused the warm coals and watched the fire die in small clouds of smoky ash and hissing steam. I slacked off the guy ropes a little against the damp of the night. Then I took off my shirt and shoes and went into the tent. I lay down on my stretcher, pulled the sheet over me, lit a cigarette and lay back, watching the small hypnotic glow of the tobacco tip in the darkness.

From the other side of the tent came a small, uncertain voice. "Renn?"

"Yes?"

"Thank you."

"No need to thank me. I did what I wanted to do."

"Thank you for that, too."

I said in a flat voice, "Do you want a cigarette?"

"Yes, please, Renn."

I threw back the sheet, crossed the tent, handed her a cigarette, then lit it for her. In the brief flare of the match her face looked like an old cameo, timelessly beautiful. I stood looking down at her while the flame burnt down and scorched my fingers. Then I threw it on the floor and kicked sand over it. I said bluntly, "Tomorrow you'd better go back to your own tent."

"Yes, Renn."

"Good night."

"Good night, Renn."

I went back to bed. I drew a blanket over me because I was cold. I did not go to sleep for a long, long time.

In the morning over breakfast we made our plans. The tide was high, so our search of the rock pools for more relics of the ancient wreck would have to wait till later. There was a flat calm; we would be able to work the boat close to the reef and move gradually outwards to the extreme edge of the shelf. My training exercises had already used a third of our air bottles. We would have to conserve the rest, not only for the search, but for salvage operations if we did find the *Doña Lucia*. This worried me. Underwater work is slow. We had a big area to cover, and if I had to go down into deep water it would be slower still. Then Pat Mitchell came up with her suggestion.

We would weight the anchor cable of the workboat with pig lead from the *Wahine* ballast. We would trail it a fathom short of the shelf bottom. I would go down and cling to it and, with the motor at half speed, they would drag me along in continuous sweeps along the whole length of the search area. Given a few hours of calm, we could make our first survey of the shallow water. A fishing line attached to my belt would be held at the upper end by Johnny Akimoto, and if the lines fouled or I wanted to stop and examine a given area, or if danger threatened, I could tug on the line and signal. It was simple, time-saving and economical. Pat Mitchell was childishly gratified when we agreed to it.

Leaving Pat to hobble about cleaning the dishes and tidying the camp, Johnny and I took the workboat out to the *Wahine*. Johnny fastened the pig lead into a bag of heavy fishnet and secured it at the top with stout cord. We took fresh air bottles from the crates—three sets— enough for four hours' work, with a little to spare for safety. Then Johnny took one of the rifles from the cabin locker and shoved three clips of ammunition into the pocket of his shorts.

"Just for safety, Renboss." He grinned.

Then he took out a long rod of polished wood, like the shaft of a golf club, with a barbed spearhead at the top.

"What's that for, Johnny?"

"Fish spear."

"For me?"

His teeth showed in a flashing grin.

"For me, Renboss. In case you get into trouble and I have to come down after you."

It was a grim reminder that we were engaged, not in holiday sport, but in a dangerous enterprise, with wealth or death at the end of it.

We loaded the gear into the workboat, and Johnny, meticulous as ever, oiled the outboard motor, cleaned it, primed it and filled the small tank with gasoline. Then we went back to the beach.

Pat Mitchell was waiting for us. She had made our lunch and packed it in a wooden box with a billy of cold tea. My harness and flippers were ready on the sand. She smiled happily when I acknowledged her forethought.

Desire stirred in me when I saw her standing there— small, brown and perfect, boyish in a checked shirt, open at the throat, and denim shorts, a canvas cap flopping comically over her forehead.

We loaded the boat, pushed off, started the engine and puttered across the glassy water to the channel entrance. Then I noticed two things which must have escaped me while Johnny and I were loading the gear. They were glass floats covered with fishnet, each with a small lead weight hanging on the underside.

"Marker buoys," said Johnny. "We used them for the lobster pots. Now we use them to mark where we start and where we finish. We cruise between them, working farther and farther out. When we have finished we bring them in again."

We rode easily through the channel and cruised along the reef, dropping the markers one at each end of the search area. Then we cut the engine and heaved over the anchor cable with its bag of ballast.

Now it was time to go. My stomach cramped with sudden fear. A little sweat broke out on my upper lip. I wiped it away with the back of my hand. Johnny Akimoto shot me a quick glance but said nothing. He and Pat helped me into the lung pack, and I was acutely aware of the touch of her hands, silken against my skin. I reached for the billycan and gulped big mouthfuls of cold tea. The cramps in my stomach relaxed.

"Two tugs on the line, Johnny, and I'm ready to go.

Three, if I want you to stop. Four and you come overside, fast—I'm in trouble. Clear?"

"All clear, Renboss," Johnny said, and gave me the thumbs-up sign for luck.

"Good hunting, Renn," said Pat Mitchell, and she leant forward and kissed me full on the lips.

I slipped the mask down over my eyes and nostrils, tested it and set it comfortably. I clamped my teeth round the lugs of the mouthpiece and went overside.

The weight of the belt and equipment took me down a few feet, until I could see the flat bottom of the workboat and the fins of the small propeller and, below them, stretching down into the twilight, the furry thread of the anchor cable.

I jackknifed and went down in a steep dive, following the angle of the cable. I felt the familiar pain in my sinus cavities and the relief when I swallowed and the Eustachian tubes cleared themselves. A school of harlequin fish flirted away from my descent, their tube-like bodies flashing blue and gold, their ugly faces smiling like a circus clown's. The reef was on my left, thirty feet away. Its colours were muted by the watery distance, and the waving grasses and the branching corals and the shadowy caverns gave it the look of a forest on a hillside. A small ray slipped out under my breast. His long barbed tail was as stiff as an arrow, and he moved with little flickering motions of his wing pinions.

In the shadows of the reef I saw the constant coming and going of other fish, small and large, and in the blue distance on my right I saw a mackerel school coast lazily by, flecked by the shafts of sunlight refracting through the clear water. Then I hit bottom.

There was sand under my feet—sand and small nodules and broken pillars of coral—but I could not see them. I was walking through waving grasses, green and red, and yellow and dark brown. Some of them brushed me with the touch of wet silk. Others rasped my skin like rough and scaly hands.

The ballast net at the end of the anchor cable hung clear of the bottom by perhaps four feet. I looked up and saw the shape of the boat, a pointed shadow against the surface.

I had grasped the anchor cable and was just about to signal Johnny to start the engine, when I saw the shark.

He was no more than twenty feet away, a big blue fellow, twice as long as a man. I could see the suckerfish clamped on the underside of his belly and on the upper edges of his dorsal fins. In front of his nose three striped pilot fish hung as motionless as their master.

He was watching me. His big tail fin flickered, but he did not move. I blew out a stream of bubbles, but he refused to be frightened by such childish tricks. I clung to the cable and leapt and waved my arms, clowning for him.

Still he hung there. I leapt out towards him. He moved away, then came back towards me in a long, lazy sweep that brought him a pace or two nearer.

I took firmer hold on the anchor cable and tried to reason out my situation, all the time keeping a wary eye on the big fellow, who, if he attacked, would come with the speed of an express train. I had two alternatives.

I could tug my belt line and Johnny Akimoto would come shooting down with his knife and the long fish spear. Then the shark might attack him, too. If he wounded it, there would be blood in the water and other sharks might come, scavenging like cannibals on the flesh of the wounded brother. Then, even if we escaped, work would be over for the day. This obviously was a last resort. I tried the second alternative.

I gave two tugs on the line and seconds later I heard a sudden clatter, magnified by the water, as the outboard started and the propeller spun with the meshing of the gears.

That was the end of Johnny Shark. He flicked himself round with his big caudal fin and shot off into the shadows so quickly that even the pilot fish were surprised.

I felt the anchor cable jerk and the next minute I was trailing out behind it, lying flat on my belly, as comfortable as on a feather bed, while I scanned the twilight ahead and the coral cliffs to the left and the shafts of sunlight in the deep waters on the right.

The grassy floor below me rose and fell like a country landscape. There were rounded hills and small depressions. There were small escarpments made by ridges of growing coral, but there was nothing large enough to indicate the presence of a wreck. Many things can happen to a sunken ship in coral waters. If it founders on a submerged reef, the corals will devour it, growing over it as the jungle grows over the lost temples of the Incas. If it falls on a sandy bottom, the sand will cover it, perhaps, but it will still show like the tumuli of ancient tombs. It may be that the tricks of tide and current will leave it exposed in whole or part while its metalwork is pitted and eaten by galvanic action and the sea worms bore into its timbers and the sea growths cover it with branches and plumes and the fish swim through the gaping holes of its wounds. But always, to the end of time, there will be a sign, a mark, a scar on the bottom of the sea.

I was looking for such a sign now.

The cable went slack for a moment, then wrenched me round in a wide arc. The boat had reached the first marker buoy and was heading seaward for our second traverse of the search area. After about thirty yards we turned again and headed backwards in the direction from which we had come. I looked down at the sea meadow beneath me and saw with a curious thrill that it fell away steeply about three yards to the left.

The land shelf was narrower than we had thought, and

if the *Doña Lucia* were here we must find her soon or not
at all. Without warning, a dark shadow blotted out the
sunlight streaming down from the surface. I looked up,
startled. A huge manta ray was flapping his lazy way over
my head. I watched, fascinated, while the whole ton
weight of him hung over me and then moved on with the
same easy motion as a bird uses in flight. I watched him
go, lying on my back against the course of the boat. For
perhaps ten seconds I followed him, then I rolled over
and scanned the blue twilight ahead.

Then, with the stunning shock of a monstrous revelation, I saw it—twenty yards ahead of me.

A great blunt mass heaved itself up from the sea floor
into the underwater twilight. Waving sea growths covered it. Sand and coral outcrops surrounded it like altar
steps. Shoals of fish, large and small, darted in and out of
the dark hollows of the seaweed. One side of it was a
rounded shoulder, the other a steep incline softened by
the fluid contours of the moving weed. At the foot of the
incline a short stumpy pillar was visible, festooned with
grassy growth. As the towline drew me closer, I knew
that I had made no mistake. The rounded shoulder was
the high stern of a Spanish ship. The incline was her
canting deck. The pillar was her shattered mast.

I had found the *Doña Lucia.*

Chapter Eleven

I caught at the line with my free hand and tugged it—once, twice and again. I heard the motor cut and, looking upwards, saw the last flurries of the propeller. The way of the workboat carried me onwards and over the sloping deck of the *Doña Lucia*. I loosed my hold and, blowing out air, let myself float down.

I landed, gently as a leaf, among the slimy sea grasses. But when I groped for a handhold the coralline growths and the seashells scored my palms. I took the knife from my belt and, working with a sort of frantic energy, scraped away a small area of weed and coral and clustered mollusks to reveal the spongy timber of the deck.

The riot of startled fish passed by me, unheeded, as I worked my way upwards along the edge of the slope and stopped to scrape away two centuries of sea growth from the broken timber of the handrail. Halfway up the incline was a gaping square hole fringed with brown weed. I looked in but withdrew in sudden fear from the blackness and tore the skin from my hands on the coral crust on the edge. I had not counted on finding our ship so quickly. I had forgotten to bring the flashlight. But now that we knew where she was there would be a time, and times, to see all that she had to show us.

At the top of the slope was a high canted platform and

above that another, smaller and narrower. On the top of the shoulder was a small structure that would probably show itself as the finial ornament of the high Spanish poop deck.

It was a triumphant moment. But I needed someone to share the triumph with me. I jerked four times on the line and, before I had counted five seconds, Johnny Akimoto came cleaving down like an avenging angel, with the spear in his hand.

I danced for him on the ancient deck. I pointed and waved my hands in clownish gestures, mumbling helplessly against the gag of the mouthpiece.

When he saw the reason for my madness Johnny clasped his hands above his head and drew back his lips in a grin. Then he swam close to me and clasped my shoulder and I saw his eyes wide with wonder behind the goggles. Then he kicked upwards, motioning me to follow him.

I staged upwards more slowly, remembering, just in time, the lessons I had learnt, knowing that even a treasure ship is poor payment for the crippling agonies of the bends.

Pat and Johnny hauled me into the boat, and the next minute we were shouting and slapping one another on the back and laughing like idiots and Pat was kissing me and I was kissing her, with the boat rocking dangerously beneath us.

It was Johnny Akimoto who recalled us to sanity.

"Before we drift, Renboss, we should take bearings, so we find this place easily again."

"Right you are, Johnny. There's too much work to do now, without trawling all over the ledge every time we want to go down."

We did a simple triangulation, lining one of the peaks with a tall pandanus and the other with a jutting rock that Pat named the Goat's Head. We tested our method by sailing round in a wide sweep and then trying to set ourselves in the diving spot. Then, more for a monument than for any sort of reliable marker, we hauled in one of the glass buoys and dropped it over the resting place of the *Doña Lucia*.

I wanted to go down again before lunch, but Johnny Akimoto shook his head.

"No, Renboss. No more today."

I protested vigorously.

"To hell with it, Johnny. We've got the whole afternoon yet."

"Johnny's right, you know, Renn," said Pat Mitchell calmly. "You've done in half a day what you were quite prepared to spend days and weeks doing. Besides, what more can you do down there today?"

"I want to have a look at that hold."

"You've got no light, Renboss," said Johnny mildly. "Besides, I can tell you what's in that hold now."

"Treasure chests, Johnny?" I grinned at him.

"No," said Johnny slowly, "not treasure chests."

"What then?"

"Water, Renboss. Water and fish and sand . . . tons and tons and tons of sand."

I was shocked into silence. My triumph was destroyed, like a pricked bubble.

"It's true, you know, Renn." Pat Mitchell laid a sympathetic hand on my knee. "That's what happens to all wrecks, isn't it? The sand piles up, round and inside them. You expected that, didn't you?"

I shook my head glumly. "I should have, but I didn't. I was so set on finding the damn ship that I didn't give half a thought to what would happen when we did find it. Well . . . what do we do now?"

"We have lunch," said Pat promptly.

From her wooden box she produced thick sandwiches of beef and damper, biscuits spread with tinned butter and cheese, and four bars of creamy chocolate. She poured tea from the billycan into our tin mugs and, as we ate and drank, rocking the ground swell, we talked.

"Renboss," said Johnny deliberately, "today we have found our ship. That is the first thing and the biggest thing. What we saw down there, you and I, shows us that her nose is well down in the bank. Something less than half of her is showing. I ask you this. You know about these things. She was carrying gold. Where would she carry it?"

"My guess, Johnny, is the stern, in the captain's quarters, under the poop deck. When we get back to shore I'll draw you a picture . . . show you what a ship of this kind looks like."

"So, then," said Johnny, "our first chance—our only chance—is that the treasure is still in the stern of the ship under the first layers of sand."

"That's right."

"If it is anywhere else, then we can never reach it, except, perhaps, with a salvage ship, which might pump away the sand. Even then"—he shrugged and spread his hands—"these things do not always succeed. You know that."

Pat Mitchell had been listening carefully. Her dark intelligent eyes were alert and questioning.

"You've got something in your mind, Johnny. What is it?"

"It is this, Miss Pat," said Johnny. "Renboss here, and myself, we know little about these things. I am useless, because I am only a diver. I learnt to work naked on the trochus beds, but I cannot stay down long enough to be of any use. Renboss, here, has learnt to dive and explore. He knows little more than that."

It was all too true. I had no answer to the relentless logic of the islander.

Pat Mitchell questioned him again.

"What do you suggest, Johnny?"

"Renboss, here, has a friend . . . the man who made these things for him."

Pat looked at me. I nodded.

"That's right . . . Nino Ferrari. He was a frogman with the Italian navy during the war."

"So you see," Johnny went on, eagerly, with his exposition, "this man is a professional. He understands salvage. He knows the tools we need and how to use them. Renboss tells me he has promised to come if we need him. I say we need him now."

Johnny again. Johnny the lost man, the alien man, with a first-class brain ticking over behind his shiny dark forehead.

I grinned at him and clapped him on the shoulder.

"All right, Johnny, that's it. Let's have ourselves a picnic. You sail us over to Bowen first thing tomorrow morning. I'll telephone Nino Ferrari in Sydney and tell him to get up here as quick as he can, with all the equipment he can lay his hands on. While we're there we'll freight the empty air bottles down to Brisbane to be refilled. What do you say, Captain?"

Johnny's dark face beamed.

"I say yes, Renboss. We take Miss Pat?"

"We take Miss Pat."

"Good. Then I show her my *Wahine* and how she sails, eh?"

From then on it was a light-hearted meal. And when it was finished we tossed our scraps overside to feed the fishes and washed our mugs in the water and stowed our gear and hauled up the ballast cable.

Then we saw the plane.

It was an old Dragon Rapide, like the barnstormers use on the country fields and the outback cattlemen charter when they can't get through in the rainy season. It came from the west—from the direction of Bowen. It was flying low and we could hear it chattering like an ancient chaffcutter. As he neared the island the pilot

banked and made a wide circuit that took him round the
cliffside and then back towards us round the edge of the
reef. He was flying on the deck, and we saw his face and
the face of his single passenger, blurred behind the cabin
window. Then he was past us, banking again for another
circuit of the island. This time he flew low over the
beach, then made a figure eight round the back of the
island and swung out again for another look at the reef
and ourselves. After that he sheered off and headed back
to the mainland.

The three of us looked at each other.

"That," said Pat with a smile, "would be a wealthy
tourist."

"That," I said grimly, "could be Manny Mannix."

Johnny's mouth was shut in a tight line. He didn't say
anything.

"Who's Manny Mannix, Renn?"

"Tell you later," I said briefly. "Come on, Johnny, let's
go home."

Johnny spun the starter wheel and the engine stut-
tered into life. We turned and headed home, through
the lazy water.

That night, for the first time in years, I held hands in
the moonlight with a girl. We sat in a small grassy hollow
sheltered from the breeze and leant our backs against a
bank of springy turf. Around us the spidery roots of the
pandanus made a trelliswork for privacy. High above us
their broad-bladed leaves made a muted clatter when
the wind moved them. Above us a white ginger blossom
spread its heavy perfume and a bank of wild orchids
drooped from a rocky ledge. The sea was a murmuring
voice and a thin ribbon of silver beyond the rim of our
retreat.

We were uneasy at first. We talked banally to conceal
our thoughts and made small jokes and laughed like
strangers who had met at a cocktail party. Then, as the

languid night relaxed us and the sea voices sang, we drew close to each other and talked more quietly of things that lie near to the heart. I told her of my brief, beautiful love for Jeannette . . . of how I came to the island . . . of why I had left it . . . of all the restless, barren years between my leaving and my coming back.

I told her the things I feared and the things I hoped. I told her of the eerie, teeming world under the water. I told her of my small odyssey in search of the *Doña Lucia* and of the morning's adventure with the shark. Her hand tightened on mine and I felt her shiver a little, as if someone had walked over her grave.

Then, shifting her position, she squatted in front of me and looked at me squarely.

"Renn, I want you to tell me something."

"What?"

"Are you really interested in money?"

It looked like thin ice. I tried to skate away from it.

"Isn't everybody interested in money?"

"Everybody needs money, Renn. Most people would like to have more of it than they have. But not everybody makes a lifetime hobby of it."

I couldn't quarrel with that. I couldn't but admire the shrewd probing of my small dark lady.

"Would it matter to you whether I were interested in money or not?"

"Yes, Renn, it would." She was earnest now, almost pleading. "I know what you want to do. I know what you think: if you can raise the treasure it will buy you freedom from a life you hate. It may—I doubt it."

"What then?"

"I think it will put gyves on your hands and chains round your heart."

Her voice was so bitter, there was so much pain in her eyes, that I was shocked. I drew her down on the bank beside me. I tried to jolly her.

"Here now, sweetheart. What is this? A sermon on the seven deadly sins?"

She blazed at me, "Yes! If you look at it that way. Look at it my way, and it isn't a sermon at all. It's—it's something I hate and fear."

"What? Money? The thing we work fifty weeks of the year for?"

"No, Renn. Not money. But the greed for it. The horrible, twisted yearning. The fear and hate I saw in your eyes this morning when you looked up at that plane and thought of Mannix."

The blade was out of the velvet now. I felt it prick painfully against my heart. I didn't relish the feeling. I said, curtly, "Greed? Hate? Fear? What the hell do you know about these things?"

"A great deal, Renn," she said simply. "I lived with them for twenty years. My father's a very rich man, and he's never had a happy moment in his life."

There was nothing to say to that. My irritation died. I said gently, "Is that all?"

She faced me, eyes bright, chin tilted proudly.

"No, Renn, not all. For the first time in my life I've met a man I can respect and admire—even love, if he would let me. I want him to fight, to stretch out his strength for a prize. But if he loses it I'd like to see him smile, so that I could still be proud of him. It's out now, Renn. Shall we go?"

"Damned if we'll go!"

I caught her in my arms and crushed her to me. I kissed her and her lips were willing. She clung to me and her body leapt and her brown arms were strong.

The sea was suddenly dumb. The stars were blotted out. And if the moon tumbled over the rim of chaos, we did not see it.

Next morning Johnny took us across to Bowen in the *Wahine*. A light wind was blowing offshore, and Johnny nursed the *Wahine* into it with skill and a naïve pride in himself and his boat. It was a picnic sailing on an easy sea under a clear sky. But when we came to Bowen the town was sweltering in the midday heat and the dust rose in little puffs about our feet as we walked from the jetty into the main street.

Johnny strode over to the garage, swinging a pair of oil cans, to buy diesel fuel. Pat had purchases of her own to make and she left me to walk over to the post office and telephone Nino Ferrari in Sydney.

The trunk service was better this morning, and twenty minutes after I had lodged my call I was talking, cautiously, to Nino Ferrari.

"Nino, this is Renn Lundigan."

"Trouble, Renn? So early?"

Nino's voice sputtered over the cables, but I caught the tension in it.

"No, Nino. No trouble yet. That comes later, possibly. I don't want to say too much. You ask the questions, I'll answer them. We've found her, Nino."

"Found her? The ship?" Nino's voice was a high, distorted squeak.

"That's right."

"How deep?"

"Ten fathoms."

"How much of her?"

"About half. The stern half."

"Sand or coral?"

"Sand."

"Much?"

"Lots of it, Nino. Lots and lots of it."

I could almost hear the cogs whirring in Nino's methodical brain.

"I get it, my friend. I get it. You want me to come up?"

"Yes, as soon as you can. Bring whatever gear you want with you. I'll pay the air freight."

"There's a little gear—not much. If we cannot do it

with that, then we cannot handle it without a big
operation. Understand?"

"I understand. Could you get up here this evening?"

Nino hesitated a moment. Then he chuckled and said
crisply, "Where is 'here'?"

"Bowen. There's an evening plane out of Sydney. Can
you make it?"

Nino chuckled again.

"You work fast, my friend."

"I have to, Nino. We may have . . . er . . . inter-
ruptions."

"Then I had better come prepared, eh?"

"It might be a good idea at that. We'll pick you up with
your gear at the airport. We'll go straight down to the
ship. That's all, Nino. If you miss the plane send me a
telegram at the airport."

"I'll do that," said Nino. "*Arrivederci.*"

"Good-bye, Nino. Make it snappy."

I hung up. As I walked out of the booth I jostled a man
in a white tropic suit who was leaning against the wall of
the next one. When I turned to apologize, he took the
cigar out of his mouth and grinned at me.

"Nice work, Commander," said Manny Mannix.

Chapter Twelve

Manny stuck the cigar back in his mouth and blew a cloud of smoke full in my face. Then he took it out again. His lips were smiling, but his cold eyes measured me with the familiar veiled huckster's stare. He was still lounging back against the door of the empty phone booth. He was relaxed and watchful as a cat.

"So you found her, eh, Commander?" he said softly.

"I tell you, Manny . . ."

He waved his cigar. "Save it, Commander. Save it. This is business. You've found her. I saw you yesterday working outside the reef. You were just telephoning to a friend to bring some gear up from Sydney. Check?"

"Check, Manny," I said quietly. "Check something else, too. If you try to move in on this deal, I'll kill you."

"Nuts!" said Manny Mannix. "Why don't you get wise to yourself, Commander? We could make a split."

"No, Manny."

Manny shrugged indifferently and blew out another cloud of smoke.

"O.K.! I buy you out. Two thousand. Cash on the barrelhead. Plus your expenses to date. Take it or leave it. If you don't, I move in and move you out. Well, Commander?"

Out of the corner of my eye I saw Johnny Akimoto mount the steps in front of the post office. I heard him put down the oil cans with a clatter. I beckoned him and he came and stood beside me.

"Look at this man, Johnny," I said gently. "Look at him and remember his face. You may possibly meet him again. His name is Manny Mannix."

There was a deadly hate in Johnny's dark eyes as he towered over Manny Mannix and looked down at him as if he were some noxious animal. When he spoke his voice was like silk.

"Stay out of this, Mr. Mannix. Stay out of this."

Manny shifted his feet a little and tossed his cigar onto the sidewalk.

"Back to the kitchen, black boy," he said easily, and put one hand on Johnny's chest to thrust him away.

Johnny caught his wrist with one hand in a grip that made Manny's eyes pop and his mouth drop open and great beads of sweat start out on his sallow cheeks. "I have never yet killed a man," said Johnny precisely, "but I think it very possible that I shall have to kill you, Mr. Mannix."

His hold relaxed and Manny's hand dropped at his side, nerveless. Then we left him. Johnny picked up his oil cans and we walked down the street to meet Pat Mitchell. Our thoughts were written on our faces, and she questioned us with instant concern.

"Renn! Johnny! What's happened?"

We told her.

"But what can he do?"

"He can do a lot things, sweetheart. We have no water rights. We have no salvage rights, either, because we haven't registered a claim. He can do just what he threatens—move in and move us out."

"By force?"

"Yes."

"But you're not doing anything wrong. Can't you claim police protection?"

"From what? Manny hasn't done anything wrong

either—yet. We'd only make fools of ourselves. More than that, we could find ourselves in a legal tangle that might take years to unravel. . . . The laws of salvage and treasure trove have kept the lawyers in pin money for centuries. You see?"

"Yes, Renn, I see."

There was a sadness in her voice that made me remember our talk of the evening before. I turned to Johnny.

"Any thoughts, Johnny?"

"No thoughts, Renboss. Only this. Your friend arrives tonight with his equipment. We meet him. We take him back to the island and start work."

"And after that?"

"We wait and see, Renboss . . . we wait and see."

Fear and depression lay over us as the heat lay over the sleepy tropic town. We walked slowly back to the jetty, unmoored the dinghy and rowed out to the *Wahine*, riding sleepily at anchor.

Johnny spread an awning over the forward hatch cover and we lay under it, sipping iced beer, eating sandwiches, talking, smoking, dozing, as the afternoon wore itself out into the slackness of evening. Always the subject of our thoughts was the same—Manny Mannix.

"I don't understand how he found us so easily," said Pat.

"Very simple, Miss Pat," said Johnny. "He knows in Sydney that Renboss has won enough money to begin his search. He knows there is an island. So far he does not know where it is. But the airlines tell him when a passenger named Lundigan leaves for Brisbane. The Lands Department in Brisbane collects a fee of two shillings and sixpence and tells him Renn Lundigan, Esquire, has bought the lease of an island latitude this and longitude that. The rest is a matter of common sense. He knows Renboss must have a boat. He knows the boat can put in at one of the ports convenient to the

island. He comes to Bowen because there is an airfield
and he can charter a plane and begin his inquiries. It is
just unfortunate that he should have come to the post
office at the same time as Renboss was making his
telephone call."

"Put it that way, it's easy, isn't it?"

"Too easy," I growled. "Too damned easy for a smart
operator like Manny."

"I am trying to think, Renboss, what he will do next."

"So am I, Johnny. There are a dozen things he could
do. But what he will do is something else again. Manny
knows too many people—can buy too many people. He
doesn't have to bid till he's stacked the deck just the way
he wants it."

"So we just wait," sighed Pat.

"We wait," said Johnny.

"Damned if we wait!" I snapped. "Johnny, can you
make the channel at night?"

Johnny gave me a sharp look, thought a moment and
then nodded.

"Yes, Renboss, I can make it. The moon is later
tonight."

"Good. Then we pick up Nino Ferrari at the airport,
come back on board and raise anchor straightaway. We
start work first thing in the morning. Even Manny
Mannix can't work that fast."

The plane landed at twenty past ten. Nino Ferrari
stepped off it—a small, compact, eager man in a light
suit and an open-necked shirt. We collected his lug-
gage—a small suitcase and three wooden crates. We
lashed the crates on the carrier of an ancient taxi which
rushed us down to the jetty at breakneck speed over the
broken and rutted roads.

By midnight we were in open water, with Johnny at
the helm and the rest of us dangling our legs in the
cockpit beside him, while we discussed the situation.

Pat's dark eyes flashed approval of Nino's crisp, professional exposition.

"First, you must understand, there will bo no miracles. You have a whole ship full of sand. Even a salvage vessel with heavy pumping equipment could not shift so much."

"We understand that, Nino."

"Good. Our best hope is that the treasure chests are in the exposed stern of the ship, near enough to the surface of the sand for us to dig them out with our hands."

This was disappointing. I said as much.

Nino answered trenchantly. "You thought I would come up here with a little box of tricks that would blow away a hundred tons of sand when I pressed a button. No. That is a schoolboy dream. This is what I have brought. Extra air bottles, because we must work long hours, two at a time, below water. Flashlights with battery replacements. And limpet mines and fuses."

"Limpet mines?" Pat was wide-eyed.

"Those I will explain in a moment. First, you will tell me, Renn, is there a current down there by the ship?"

"Yes, there is. It sets along the direction of the reef and crosswise to the way the ship is lying."

"Strong?"

"Moderate."

"*Ebbene*. . . . Now I will tell you. Your friend, Johnny here, will understand better than you what I try to explain."

Johnny turned his head and acknowledged the compliment with a wide smile. They would work well together, these two. Nino Ferrari went on. . . .

"You will remember that when you first saw this ship you saw that the sand was piled about its sides. You did not go into the hold because the water was too dark. But when you do go into it, with the flashlights, you will see that the sand is piled up there also—but it is continually in motion. You understand that?"

I nodded.

"Now, this is how we work. We explore first the area that is out of the sand. If we find nothing, we go down into the hold. We dig there—all over it. . . ."

"With our hands?"

"With our hands. We are under water, you see. We raise too much sand, it floats about us and obscures our view. Best then to work quietly."

"And if we don't find anything in the hold, Nino, what then?"

"Then," said Nino, "we use the mines. They are small, because we are dealing with an old wooden ship and we don't want to blow her to pieces. We fix the mines, one on either side of the hull, and detonate them with a time fuse. They will blow holes in the side of the hull and the current will remove at least part of the sand inside. You see?"

It was not hard to see. Nino's trenchant phrases spoke of confidence and experience. Our courage, sadly shrunken after our meeting with Manny Mannix, grew again to man size, but Nino wasn't finished yet.

"This I want you to understand clearly. This is the last stage of the operation. If, after the mines, we go down and find nothing, we ourselves can do no more. If you want to go farther, you must think of a salvage expedition with heavy equipment. I tell you this because you must not have false hopes. They are costly and dangerous."

I told him that we understood. I told him that so far as diving operations were concerned we would work to his orders. Then I told him about Manny Mannix.

Nino's dark eyes snapped fire and he snorted contemptuously. "This I have seen often before. There is a smell of gold and all the vultures come flapping as if to a dead body. Sometimes there are dead bodies. So I brought this."

He fished in his pocket and brought out a small blue Beretta that gleamed dully in the starlight. He sighed.

"I hope I never have to use it. I came to this country to find peace. But where gold is, there is never peace."

I knew Pat was looking at from the other side of the cockpit, but I dared not meet her level eyes.

It was after midnight and we had a three-hour run ahead of us. If we wanted to make an early start in the morning we would have to snatch what sleep we could. I took the wheel from Johnny and sent the three of them below to rest. When I raised the island I would wake Johnny and he would make the tricky passage through the reef.

Before she went, Pat put her arms round my neck and kissed me.

"Good night, sailorman."

"Good night, sweetheart."

Then I was alone. I heard the brief murmur of their voices as my friends and my lover settled themselves to sleep. I saw the cabin light extinguished and caught, through the open door, the small red glow of Nino's cigarette. Then that, too, went out, and the night was mine and all the wonder of wind and stars and bellying white sail.

In the morning Nino Ferrari took command of our small company. He squatted on the sand in front of the big tent, the sun gleaming on his small muscular body. He gave his orders simply and bluntly.

"First we must dive from the *Wahine*. The workboat is too small."

I looked across at Johnny. He nodded agreement.

"All right with me, Renboss. I run her wherever you want."

Nino went on, "We keep all our stores on board—lungs, bottles, lamps—all of it. We keep a day's food and water on board and the medicine chest, in case there are accidents."

"I'll look after that part of it," said Pat.

Nino nodded briefly and continued, "We are working

in ten fathoms. That is not too bad. We will work for half an hour at a time, then come up and rest for two hours before going down again."

This sounded like an expensive waste of time. I queried the point. Nino answered me without rancour. "If we were working in deeper water I should say only fifteen minutes' work and three hours of rest."

"But why?"

"Because to this point you have been diving only. You have not been working. When you work under water the exertion causes a greater and a quicker discharge of nitrogen into the bloodstream. The danger of the bends is therefore greater. This way we diminish risk and fatigue."

"We'll do as you say, of course. I just wanted to know. But couldn't we save time if we went down singly and worked that way? One man resting—the other working?"

Nino's bright eyes twinkled ironically.

"If you were an experienced diver, I would say yes, by all means. But you are not. It is better that we work together—better and safer."

I grinned submission. Then I asked another question, "How do we tell the time?"

"I have a watch," said Nino, "a watch that the makers say will work under water. But when one is busy it is easy—and dangerous—to forget time. So Johnny here will fire a bullet into the water for a signal. The noise when it strikes the water will be very clear down below. When we hear it we come up."

"What happens if you find anything down there?" asked Pat.

"For small things there is a weighted fish basket, which Johnny lets down on a line each time we descend. For big things like"—Nino grinned broadly—"like a treasure chest, we put a sling under it and haul it on board. . . . Now, if there are no more questions, we should take the gear aboard and get to work."

"I've got a simple question," said Pat. "It's got nothing to do with diving. Where does Nino sleep?"

It was Johnny Akimoto who answered that one—a little too quickly, I thought, though I could not imagine why.

"Nino sleeps in the big tent with Renboss. I will sleep aboard the *Wahine*."

And that was that. A simple question, a simple answer, with no dark thoughts behind them. I could not even tell myself why they worried me.

Forty minutes later the *Wahine* was anchored outside the reef, with the *Doña Lucia* sixty feet under her keel.

Nino Ferrari and I sat on the hatch cover drinking strong sugared tea, while Johnny spliced a cord handle on a fish basket and Pat squatted native-fashion beside me, listening to Nino's final instructions.

"When we go into the hatch you will have to be careful. Outside the light you will not be able to see very much. But remember there will be beams, covered with coral and shellfish, and small projections of all kinds. Brush against them and you may cut your breathing tubes."

The same thought had occurred to me. It wasn't a happy prospect. Pat shivered with excitement at the thought of the nameless terrors of the world she had never seen. She turned to Nino.

"What about the other things, Nino? The sharks and . . . and . . ."

Nino laughed. "And the monsters that they show you on the films? There are monsters in the deeps, yes, but they do not normally live in the holds of ships. There are fish that are dangerous to the diver, just as there are animals that are dangerous to him on land. But for the most part the fish is as wary of the diver as he is of them.

For the rest"—he crossed himself simply—"the hand of God reaches down even into the great waters."

"'They that do business in great waters, these see the works of the Lord and His wonders in the deep.'"

The quotation came simply and surprisingly from the girl at my side.

"'They cry to the Lord in their trouble and He brings them out of their distress.'" Nino added the tag in liquid Italian, then smiled and stood up. "Time to go down, my friend. Harness up."

We buckled on our gear and went overside, steadying ourselves on a cleated rope. This time I had a large flat rubber-sealed flashlight with a big reflector clipped on my belt. We swam round to the anchor cable and followed it down into the blue twilight. Nino was behind me as we went down, and I looked back to see him give me a small signal of approval. Then we were on the bottom, two men-fish standing in a waving meadow whose grasses were stirred by a soundless wind. The wreck of the *Doña Lucia* was thirty feet away, straight ahead of us.

I swam over to Nino and floated beside him. I touched his shoulder and pointed eagerly. He grinned behind his mask and gave me a thumbs-up. Then we saw Johnny's weighted basket sliding down to us through the twilight, and we moved off.

I led Nino up the sloping weed-covered deck and showed him the dark gaping hole with its fringe of weeds. He shone the flashlight into the blackness, and in the pool of light I saw a waving of red sea grasses, the naked arms of small branch coral and a cavalcade of small bright fish, which swam leisurely out of the light into the surrounding darkness.

Nino snapped off the flashlight and motioned me upwards. At the top of the incline, under the first canted platform, there was a bulkhead, broken by a door which was now no more than a narrow dark hole fringed with weeds. Nino flashed the light again, snapped it off after a brief scrutiny and went on again. Whether the opening led to cabin or companionway we could not tell—yet.

The bulkhead on the first platform was similarly broken. But the opening led this time obviously to a cabin. Possibly the captain's. This would be our first area of search after we had completed the survey of the poop. The next deck area was narrow and surrounded by carved bulwarks and surmounted by some sort of finial carving. I should have liked to scrape away the weeds and barnacles and coral to examine it more closely, but our time and our air supply and our strength were all limited. We could not spend them on antiquarian trifles.

Then Nino took control. Motioning me to follow him, he turned and swam downwards to the cabin deck and waited for me outside the narrow black entrance.

It was an eerie moment. I had subdued, by practice, my first fears of the twilight world under the water . . . subdued but not destroyed them. Now they came trooping back full-size with new fears added—fear of the darkness, fear of the unknown monsters that might lurk where the light did not shine. My flesh broke out in goose pimples again. Then Nino smiled behind his mask and laid his hand on my shoulder in a gesture of reassurance. He snapped on the flashlight.

There were no monsters. There were only fish. Fish and weeds and water and beyond them a new darkness which my own flashlight would help to dissipate. I switched it on and followed Nino through the festooned weeds into the cabin.

Out of the corner of my eye I saw a pair of big round eyes staring at me and a round, thick-lipped mouth that slobbered continually. I whirled and flashed the light.

It was a big blue groper. He flicked his tail and swung off into the shadows. Nino turned and signalled me to come beside him. We stood together on the sandy

uneven floor and played our lights on the wall of sea
growth ahead of us.

To me, the novice, it was a disappointing sight. There
were projections that might have been beams. There
was a recess that might have been a bunk alcove. There
was a shapeless mass, waist-high, that might have been a
cabin table. Beyond that—nothing . . . nothing but
the shifting outlines of weeds and sea grasses and the
flutter of small fish in and out of their roots.

We turned the light upwards. Hanging weeds brushed
our faces. I put up my hand and felt the faint outline of a
beam under the slimy growth. I shone the light ahead of
it and saw a large incrustation that looked vaguely like a
hanging lamp. I struck at it with my knife. It snapped off
and dropped slowly and weightlessly to the sandy floor.

Nino made an impatient gesture that said, "Leave it,"
and knelt down on the weed-covered sand.

I did the same. I saw him scraping with his knife
among the weeds and sand and coral stumps. He was
testing the depths of incrustation over the planks.
Eighteen inches down we struck wood, pulpy and
waterlogged.

Nino stood up and made a gesture of negation. No
treasure chests can be hidden under eighteen inches of
sand. Nino then moved over to the far corner of the
cabin where the slope of the floor had caused the sand to
pile up into larger and deeper drifts.

A canny professional, Nino. He knew his business. He
went down on his knees again and began scraping the
sand away with knife and hands, probing carefully ahead
with his fingers. I chose a spot three feet away from him
and began to work in the same fashion.

I had not been digging for more than three minutes
when my hand struck something that was unmistakably
wood. I shifted the flashlight, but I could see nothing.

Sudden fever took possession of me and I started
digging frantically, like a dog for a buried bone. In an

instant Nino was beside me, wagging his finger in a reproving gesture, showing me in dumb show that this was a dangerous way to work. Then he knelt down and began digging with me. The sand rose in swirls and eddies above us, blinding us. No sooner had we clawed out a handful than two more flowed in to fill the space we had left. But, after an interminable labour, we managed to clear enough to identify my find.

It was the brassbound corner of an old sea chest.

At that precise moment we heard a crack that sounded like the snapping of a tree branch. It was the warning shot. Time to return to the surface.

I looked at Nino. I pointed to the box. I made gestures, pleading with him to stay down a little longer. He shook his head. His eyes were grim behind the mask.

"Topside!" he signalled.

Slowly, terribly slowly, we staged upward to the *Wahine*, while the sand settled once more round the sea chest in the *Doña Lucia*.

Chapter Thirteen

Nino and I stretched on mattresses under the canvas awning amidships. Pat served us cool beer and cigarettes, while Johnny, singing in the galley, prepared the pashas' meal—fillets of red emperor, caught while we were at the bottom of the sea, fritters of sliced bully beef and potato chips, canned peaches and preserved cream, fresh from the icebox. We must eat well, rest well. So Nino had ordered, so it was done.

And, as we lay there in the warm shade, rocked by the gentle swing of the sea, Nino read me lesson number two.

"You are a damn fool, Renn. After all I tell you about the way to work under water, you scrabble and scratch like a child looking for a lost toy. You work slowly, man . . . slowly. You save your air and your strength and you keep the nitrogen poison down as low as possible. Think you are making love to your girl here." He cocked a wicked eye at Pat, who blushed and retreated to the galley. ". . . Gently, gently. You reach the same end in the same time. And the going is much more pleasant."

"All right, Nino. Round one to you. But why the blazes couldn't we have stayed down a little longer? We'd have had that box clear in ten minutes."

Nino heaved himself up on his elbow and jabbed an

accusing finger at me. His eyes flashed. His anger was theatrical.

"So! The young cock wants to crow his own song, eh? Let me tell you something, smart one. You know how long it will take us to uncover that box? Fifteen—twenty minutes. You know what would have happened if we had stayed down? We would have needed another twenty minutes to stage up, another hour to rest. And still no box. Why? Because there was no sling ready to lift it up. When we go down this time, the sling follows us; and if we are lucky—if we are lucky, I repeat—we may get the box up in time."

"And if we don't?"

"Then we leave it," retorted Nino. "Do you think the fish will eat it? Do you think a mermaid will tuck it under her flipper and walk off with it?"

He clapped his free hand to his forehead with a gesture of contempt and despair and rolled back onto his pillow. There was a roar of laughter from Pat and Johnny who had watched Nino's triumphant little drama from the safety of the cockpit.

Then dinner was served and, while we were eating, Pat put the question direct to Nino Ferrari.

"This box you've found. Is there any chance of its being a treasure box?"

Nino shrugged eloquently.

"Who knows, *signorina*? Maybe yes—maybe no. In my experience of these things, it is generally no. It is as well not to build up too many hopes. From the look of that cabin down there I should say we will not find too much. If we went scavenging through the rubbish, we might find small things—a drinking cup, a knife, a pewter plate. But they would be hard to distinguish under the growth and not worth the trouble." He grinned engagingly. "I'm sorry to disappoint you, *signorina*, but this business of treasure hunting is one long disillusion. I knew a man who made a fortune when he salvaged a load of plastic sheets. I knew another who found a treasure ship—a real one, too—and lost his whole fortune because he couldn't pump the mud away as fast as the sea could spread it."

Johnny Akimoto nodded his approval. This small, dark fellow from Genoa was a man after his own heart. The sea had spawned them both and they were both wise in her ancient ways. Then Johnny's face clouded with sudden recollection. He hesitated a moment, then he spoke.

"Renboss, Miss Pat thought I should not tell you this while you are working. I think now that I should tell you."

"Let's have it, Johnny."

"While you were working down there, the airplane came again."

"The same plane?"

"The same plane. The same movement. Round the island twice, three times. Then home again."

"Hell and damnation!"

I leapt up from my mattress. Nino Ferrari pulled me down again.

"If you want to go down this afternoon, you stay where you are. What has happened that is new? You know this Manny fellow will spy on your work. No sense to spoil the work because you are angry with the spy."

Reluctantly I lay down again. I was boiling with anger. Johnny's next words echoed my own thought.

"I think this time it is more serious than the last."

"Why, Johnny?"

It was Pat's voice this time, questioning, earnestly.

"Because, Miss Pat, this time he sees the *Wahine* instead of the workboat. He knows that we have begun to work the wreck. He knows that whatever he plans to do must be done quickly."

I turned to Nino. "Johnny's right, you know. Manny can't delay too much longer. We've got to move faster."

Nino waved an eloquent hand. "Can we work any faster than we are working now? Can we do any more than we have planned to do? No. So why spoil your own digestion and mine? Today we work the cabin. Tomorrow we work the hold. We keep on working until this Manny fellow turns up—"

"Sure, sure! And what do we do when he does turn up?"

"I think maybe if we use our brains instead of our bottoms we give him the surprise of his life."

Nino chuckled and closed his eyes, and not another word could I get out of him until it was time to go down again.

We checked the pressure in our air bottles and tested the regulators, and while Pat helped us to harness up, Johnny tied the ballast net on the end of the long sling cable. This would go down with us. We would carry the cable end over to the wreck and dump the ballast bag inside the door of the cabin. Then, when we had uncovered the box, Johnny would haul it to the surface while we were staging up.

Before I put on my mask, Pat kissed me on the lips and said, "Good luck, Renn. And try not to be too disappointed."

"I won't. There's a treasure topside, even if there's none below."

Then I followed Nino Ferrari over the side and felt the shock of the water on my skin, warm after its two-hour broiling on the deck. The ballast bag followed us down and we carried it between us as we swam over the now familiar deck and up to the door of the cabin.

The dark held no terrors for me now. The staring fish eyes, the secret scurrying movements in the shadows, were all forgotten as I knelt with Nino on the rough floor and began steadily, rhythmically, to scrape away the sand from the sea chest. Nino watched me shrewdly and nodded his satisfaction when he saw that I had learnt my lesson.

Try to bury a kerosine can in your kitchen garden. You'll be surprised at the size of the hole you have to dig. Try to get rid of the same can six months later and you'll find you have double the work on your hands. Tackle it on a wet weekend and you'll be up to your knees in slush within ten minutes. Imagine two men attempting the same task in sixty feet of water, shifting with their bare hands two hundred years' accumulation of fluid sand and trailing seaweed and coral growths. You will understand that Nino had not exaggerated the size of the job.

I was working on the underside of the box, Nino on the upper. No sooner had I scraped away one handful of sand than more flowed down into the hole to take its place. The water around us was full of drifting particles which blurred our masks and vexed our patience. We had been working for perhaps fifteen minutes when Nino tapped my shoulder and beckoned me to look at his side of the box.

I saw it—and my heart sank. The top of the box had been stove in, probably on the night of the wreck, and the inside of it was full of sand.

The brass strips which had bound it were corroded and broken; the metal studs still left in the spongy wood were coated with coral cells and tiny mollusks. They scraped our hands as we plunged them into the box, screening the liquid sand for any trace of gold or jewels or ornaments.

My hand closed round something hard, but when I brought it up it proved to be a corroded buckle—brass, probably, or pinchbeck. Nino brought up a broken, rusted knife. This too was of common metal. When he found another buckle, larger than the first, he made a rueful mouth behind his mask and signalled me to stop. His miming told me only what I knew already.

The box was a very ordinary sea chest. It had held

nothing more valuable than its owner's shore suit and his buckled shoes and his sea knife. The voracious sea organisms had eaten everything but the knife and the buckles of his hat and shoes.

For a moment we stood looking down at our pitiful find. Then Nino motioned me to help him, and we lugged and heaved the rest of the box clear of the sand and tipped its contents out among the seaweeds on the floor. We found nothing more than a pitted metal handle with a piece of porcelain still fixed to one end.

Then we heard the smack of the bullet on the water. We tossed the box on the pile of sand in the corner and watched it settle weightlessly among the weeds.

Clutching our few childish relics in our hands, we made our hesitant way to the surface.

"Tired, Renn?"

Pat and I were sitting on the forward hatch cover while Johnny steered us home through the channel and into the lagoon, and Nino, calm as a cat, was asleep on one of the bunks. Pat's hand was in mine. Her dark head was resting against my shoulder.

"Yes, sweetheart, I'm tired. Nino was right. It's wearing work."

"Are you disappointed, Renn?"

"Yes. It's crazy and childish and I don't want any sympathy. I'm new to the business. I'll have to learn to be patient. That's all."

"Nino says you'll start working the hold tomorrow."

"That's right."

"Will it be difficult?"

"No more difficult than the cabin. Except that there's a lot more of it and the sand is ten times deeper."

"It doesn't sound very promising, does it?"

"No. It's a matter of luck, that's all."

She hesitated a moment, then went on, "Renn, I've been thinking."

"About what?"

"About the coins on the reef. Do you think it's possible that any of the crew reached the island?"

"And took the treasure boxes with them?"

"Yes."

"Sweetheart," I said patiently, "we've been over all this before. You heard what Johnny said about it. I tell you, I've been over the whole island. There's not a trace of any such happening."

"Aren't there any caves?"

"Nary a one. There are a few rock holes and overhangs on the cliffside. But they're either too shallow or too high up in the wall. There's a sort of narrow cleft up on the eastern horn. Jeannette and I looked at it once, but it was so dank and musty and full of goat smell that we didn't go inside. Apart from that, nothing . . . nothing at all."

She sighed and made a little rueful mouth.

"Well, so much for my fine theory. Looks as though it's up to you and Nino, doesn't it?"

"Yes, it's up to us."

Johnny was slacking off now and we were sliding in to anchorage. I stood up and walked forward to be ready with the hook. Pat followed me up.

"Renn?"

"Yes."

"Johnny's worried about something."

"Did he say what it was?"

"No, but he wants to talk to you tonight, Renn . . . after dinner. Alone."

I tossed the anchor overboard and the cable went whipping down after it. Then the cable tightened. The *Wahine* stopped drifting and her stern swung round into the current. The first day's work was over. We were home again.

* * *

Dinner was over. The stars hung low in a soft sky. Nino squatted beside the fire, carefully taping the hose joint of his diving gear and crooning happily to himself. Pat had gone down to her tent to write up the thesis that would make my brown girl, incongruously, a Doctor of Science. I saw her shadow cast by the lamp against the glowing canvas of the tent. Johnny was going back to the *Wahine* to sleep. I walked down with him to the beach.

When we were out of earshot of the others, Johnny told me, "Renboss, I am scared."

"Of what, Johnny?"

"Something is going to happen with this Manny Mannix."

"We know that, Johnny. We've always known it."

"Yes, Renboss, but . . ." He stumbled and groped for the words that would frame the thought and make its urgency clear to me. "How can I explain it, Renboss? It is like the old days on the trochus beds. Word would go round that this one or that one had found a new place and was working it quietly. When he walked into the bar the others would watch him silently, with greedy eyes. They would measure his strength and his courage and the loyalty of his crew. If he were strong and his men loved him, they would fawn and smile and offer him drinks and try to wheedle his secret out of him. But if he were weak or cowardly or unloved, then they would growl and mutter. Someone would start a fight. A bottle would be thrown and the shell knives would come out, and they would fight like animals. . . . This Manny is animal, Renboss. That is the way he will fight."

I nodded gravely. Johnny was right. Manny Mannix was an animal with an animal's courage. But Manny was a businessman, and where money was concerned, Manny would take no chances. If he moved at all, he would move in strength. And if you stroll round the waterfronts of the north with money in your pocket you will find plenty of tough characters who are not too particular how they earn it. Johnny watched me with troubled eyes.

"You agree with me, Renboss?"

"I agree with you, Johnny."

"What are you going to do, Renboss?"

"What do you want me to do, Johnny?"

He considered the question a long time before answering.

"For myself and for you and for this diver fellow, Nino, I would say we stay and fight. But there is the girl."

I saw the point. There was the girl. If there were violence, she would be caught in the midst of it. She would be there when the animals began to rend and tear each other. And afterwards . . . ? It was not a thing that should happen to any girl, and this was the girl I had come to love. There was only one answer.

"All right, Johnny. We send her back in the morning. If it's flat weather she can take the workboat. She needn't go to the mainland. There are two or three islands where she can put up and wait till it's over."

Johnny Akimoto straightened up. It was as if a great load had slipped from his shoulders. He smiled and shook my hand.

"Believe me, Renboss, it is best. You will not want her to go, I know that. But when she is gone you will be able to fight with free hands. . . . Good night, Renboss!"

"Good night, Johnny!"

I watched him push off the dinghy, step lightly over the stern and scull out to the *Wahine* with long, easy strokes. I turned away and walked up the beach to Pat's tent.

She got up when I entered. We kissed and clung together for a moment, then I sat her down in the chair again and perched myself on a packing case beside her. I said flatly, "Sweetheart, I'm sending you away tomorrow. There's going to be trouble. You'll take the workboat and go over to South Esk or Ladybird Island and stay there until we come for you."

She looked at me a long time without speaking; there were tears in her eyes and her lip trembled. Then she took hold of herself and asked me, calmly enough, "Do you want me to go, Renn?"

"No. I don't want you to go. I think you should go."

"And Johnny?"

"Johnny thinks the same."

She turned her face away and dabbed at her eyes with a small handkerchief. When she faced me again her mouth was firm and there was a proud lift to her chin. There was a note in her voice that I had not heard before.

"You are going to fight, aren't you, Renn?"

"Yes."

"For the treasure ship?"

"Partly . . . yes. But not only for that." Slowly, painfully, I tried to piece out for her the thought that had been growing in my mind for the past days. "I know now that we may never find the cargo of the *Doña Lucia*. There is still a chance, of course. There is an even greater chance that it may be buried so deep under the sand that we could never come to it in a million years. In that case the fight would be a monstrous and costly folly. But don't you see? It's not only that. It's all the other things. It's this—this life, my friends, this island. For the first time in my life I've stood a free man with my own land under my feet. I'll fight for that, sweetheart. I think, possibly, I will kill for it."

"And your own woman, Renn?" The words came out in a whisper. "I am your woman, aren't I?"

"You're my woman, Pat. From now to crack o' judgment."

I stood up. I reached out to draw her to me, but she pushed me gently away.

"Then I'm staying with you. You're my man, and you can't send me away."

I tried to argue with her and she closed my mouth with kisses. I tried to threaten her and she laughed in my face. I tried to charm her to submission and she dismissed me, reluctantly.

"Go to bed, Renn. Tomorrow's a working day. When this is over we'll have all the time in the world—till crack o' judgment, as you say."

I was shorn like Samson. I kissed her again and went back to my tent.

Nino Ferrari was still squatting by the fire, tinkering with the delicate mechanism of the regulators. He looked up when he heard me and gave me a crooked smile.

"A fine girl you got yourself there. She'll make a good wife for a diver. A deep-water man needs plenty of sleep."

I grunted irritably and squatted down beside him. He flipped me a cigarette.

"Something on your mind, my friend?"

"Yes. We're going to have a fight on our hands. Johnny thinks so. I think so."

Nino cocked his dark head and whistled soundlessly.

"So! It is going to be like that, eh? I have seen these things before, with the sponge fishers in the Aegean. They can be ugly. When the wine flows and the long knives come out." He jerked his thumb over his shoulder in a significant gesture. "What about the girl?"

I shrugged. "I wanted her to go, she refused. Short of running her off the island by force, there's nothing I can do about it."

Nino tightened the last screw in the regulator and folded it carefully in clean cloth to keep the sand away from it, then he put the whole apparatus back in its case and snapped the lid.

"First rule for a lung diver," he said irrelevantly.

"Clean the regulator after every dive. If it fails in deep water you are a dead man."

There was a silence between us. I heard the cheep and clack of insects in the bush behind us. I watched the dipping flight of a bat. Then I turned to Nino again.

"Out there, this morning, you said you had something we might use against Manny Mannix when he comes. What is it?"

His dark eyes gave me a long, sidelong stare. Then he bent his head and seemed to be studying the backs of his hands. When he spoke his voice was level, without emphasis.

"My friend, one does not put a knife into the hands of a child, nor a loaded pistol into the fist of a man who is angry. The knowledge that I have came to me in a sad time, a time of violence and bloody destruction. If it is necessary to use it again, I will do so. Even though you are my friend, I will say what is to be done and how, and for the consequences, I will take the responsibility. I am sorry, but this is a thing that I feel deeply—here in my heart."

And with that I had to be content. I grinned, got up, clapped him on the shoulder and took myself off to bed. I dreamt of a wartime beachhead with dead bodies rolling in the backwash and a man pinned down in a foxhole by machine-gun fire from the palms.

The man in the foxhole was myself. The man behind the gun was Manny Mannix.

Chapter Fourteen

At seven o'clock the next morning we dropped anchor in the diving area. We planned to make three dives a day and, allowing for rest periods and staging time, each dive would cost us three hours of daylight. I wanted to make four descents, but Nino was adamant. The gain would be an illusion, he said. After two days or three the strain would tell and we would begin to feel the effects of long immersion and nitrogen narcosis.

Today we were to make our first survey of the hold. We harnessed up quickly, and I felt the tenseness of expectation as I climbed overside and followed Nino down, watching his air bubbles stream upwards past my face.

Once more we swam over the waving growths of the deck until we came to the gaping hole with its fringe of slime and sharp corals. Nino motioned me to wait. I saw him dive, slanting downwards along the beam of his own flashlight. I noted the care he took to avoid fouling his airlines against the jagged edges. Then he shone his light backward, and I dived in to him along the beam.

The space in which we found ourselves was, perhaps, three times as large as the cabin we had visited the day before. The sand sloped upwards and the timbers with their coating of sea grass canted downwards wedge-fashion towards the rear of the chamber. The beam of my flashlight picked out a colony of lobsters clinging to the roof timbers in one corner. I told myself I would take one up to the *Wahine* for lunch. I felt something brush my shoulder blades. I turned sharply and flashed my light on a large squid. I saw his black parrot beak and his saucer eyes, then his tentacles stiffened beneath him and he shot upwards, leaving a puff of ink, like a ghost image, behind him.

Nino beckoned me to his side; together we made the circuit of the hold, standing where the roof was high, swimming on our backs or our bellies where the space narrowed between the sand and the timbers.

Our groping hands traced the outlines of ancient deck beams under the sleek waving growths. We marked them carefully. They would serve as guides when we came to divide the area into sections for our daily searches. When we had made the circuit, we swam back and forth across the bottom, groping with our hands among the weeds and sand and coral for anything that might resemble a box. It was superficial, unsatisfying work, but we had to do it. Later we would begin the heartbreaking task of turning over hundreds of square feet with our hands and our knives.

When we had traversed the whole area, Nino motioned me to stop. For a few minutes we hung suspended in the new element, grimacing at each other and making crazy dumb show with our hands. Then Nino signalled to me to shine my flashlight along one wall of the hold. I did so. He swam over to the corner, measured with his outstretched arms a width from the corner, then swam from that point parallel with the wall to the other end of the hold. The beam of my light followed him. I understood what he meant. He was marking out a narrow strip of sand for our first search.

He swam back to me and side by side we began to work. We scraped and scrabbled and probed, pushing

ourselves backwards with our hands while our bodies
hung suspended behind us like the bodies of fish.

We had not been working more than a few minutes
when we heard the familiar impact of a bullet on the
surface of the water. We stopped. I looked at Nino. Nino
looked at me. We had not been down more than fifteen
minutes. Then we heard a second impact and, immediately after it, a third.

Something was wrong on the *Wahine*. Nino gestured
to me. We swam out of the hold and made our way as
quickly as we dared to the surface.

Johnny and Pat hauled us aboard and, as we stood
dripping on the deck, Johnny pointed across the water,
westward.

"They're coming, Renboss," he said quietly.

She was a lugger, like the *Wahine* but bigger, broader
in the beam. Her hull was black. Her spars were bare.
She was coming under engines, fast, at about twelve
knots. She would be with us in twenty minutes.

Johnny Akimoto handed me the glasses. I focussed
and saw that her deck space was cluttered with ma-
chinery under canvas. I saw more bulky shapes forward
of the main hatch. I saw men stripped to the waist
moving round her decks. I saw a figure in a white duck
suit braced against the forward stays—Manny Mannix.

I handed Nino the glasses. He scanned the lugger for a
few moments, then lowered them.

"Diving gear," he said curtly. "Pumps and a winch. A
lot of other stuff for'ard. Could be anything."

I turned to Johnny Akimoto. "Do you know her,
Johnny?"

"Yes. She is a trochus boat, Renboss. Twin diesels.
The number says she is registered on Thursday Island."

Clever Manny. Clever, clever, Manny. Never forget a
face, never neglect a contact. Manny had chartered a
boat like this before, when he went north, with a
legitimate buyer's license to buy war surplus in the

islands. Manny had brought it back with a false manifest, loaded with gear he had plundered from forgotten dumps in a hundred lonely bays. A simple telegram would bring the same boat and the same tough skipper and the same crew of plug-uglies racing down the reef to pick him up at Bowen. And if the business turned out to be dirty business, a cut for the skipper and a bonus for the boys would guarantee Manny silence and security.

"What do you want to do, Renboss?" said Johnny.

"Wait for her, Johnny. Just sit here and wait. Stow the gear, Nino. Pat, get below and make us something to eat. If we're going to have trouble, I'd like to be fed first."

She gave me a wan smile and padded aft. Nino picked up the lung packs and began drying them carefully. Johnny Akimoto stood watching the black shape of the lugger as she raced towards us across the flat water.

As she drew closer I could see the white numerals on her bows. I could see the bearded faces and tanned bodies of her crew. I could see Manny Mannix waving his cigar as he talked. I was still puzzled by the curious shapes under the canvas in the forepeak. I pointed them out to Johnny. They meant nothing to him, either. He bent down, picked up the rifle from the hatch cover, ejected the spent shell, slid another shell into the breech and rammed the bolt home. Then he slipped on the safety catch and laid the rifle carefully in the scuppers, out of sight.

Then Pat and Nino came on deck with mugs of tea and a plate of beef sandwiches. We sat on the hatch and ate together, watching the black lugger move closer and closer. The warm sun streamed down on us through the canvas awning. The *Wahine* rocked gently in the quiet water. We might have been a fishing party, out on a picnic cruise, had it not been for the tension between us and the menacing black hull with its motley crew.

We had hardly finished our meal when they came up with us. Thirty yards to starboard they cut the motors.

The way brought her across our bows. The helmsman swung her beam to and we saw the anchor go down with a rattle and a splash. Then we were lying broadside to with no more than ten yards of water between us.

The crew lined the rail, laughing and shouting. They whistled and called ribaldries when they saw there was a woman among us. There were perhaps a dozen of them—black, white and in-between. Some were young and some were not so old. Some were bearded—others wore careless stubbly growth. But all were brown and tough and dangerous—veterans of the shabby towns on the fringe of the law.

In the midst of them stood Manny Mannix, incongruous in his white suit and his gaudy tie. His panama hat was tilted on the back of his head. The inevitable cigar was stuck in the corner of his mouth. He took it out to hail me.

"Hiya, Commander! Nice weather we're having!"

I said nothing. I felt Pat stiffen beside me.

"I'd like to come aboard, Commander. Business talk. Private."

"Stay on your own deck, Manny."

Manny waved a tolerant hand. He shouted back, "Just trying to be friendly. The market's still open if you're interested."

"I'm not interested, Manny."

"I'll split with you, Commander—fifty-fifty. Look, I've got the gear and the men to work it." He made a sweeping gesture that embraced the whole boat and her ragged crew. "If you don't like that, I'll still buy you out on the same terms."

"The answer's no, Manny. If you want it, you've got to take it."

"It's open water, Commander. Show me a salvage claim and I'll leave you to it."

"No claim, Manny. We were here first, that's all."

The men lining the deck sent up a great bellow of

laughter. I saw Johnny's hand go down to the rifle lying in the scuppers. I stopped him before he touched it.

Manny Mannix hailed me again. "I've got witnesses, Commander. Witnesses to say that I made you a fair offer for something you don't own anyway. Now I'm moving in."

I bent and picked up the rifle and showed it to him.

"I told you you'd have to fight for it, Manny."

There was another bellow of laughter. Manny swung round and called an order to a seaman standing apart in the eyes of the boat.

In an instant the canvas was thrown back. My puzzle was solved. The humped shapes were depth charges, looted from some island dump. Behind them was a small machine gun mounted on a tripod. There was a full belt in the magazine and our man had his finger on the button.

"Still want a fight, Commander?" yelled Manny.

The gallery roared at his wit. Then his face darkened and his voice took on a new, venomous note.

"I'm moving in, Commander . . . as of now. You take your boat and sail her back inside the reef and stay there. If you so much as stick your ears out before we're finished, you'll be cut down. And just in case you and your little Wop think of any frogmen's tricks—like working the bottom when my boys are resting—remember those." He pointed to the sinister metal cans lying on the forward deck. "We'll take a little run and drop 'em on you as we go."

And there it was—the royal flush. And Manny was sitting on it. The last hand and we could do nothing but watch him scoop the chips into his pocket and go home. For the second time I was broke and busted in a game with Manny Mannix.

But I wouldn't give Manny the satisfaction of hearing me say it. Out of the corner of my mouth I spoke to Nino and Johnny.

"Nino, get the anchor up. Johnny, get the engines started, and we'll take her home. Don't hurry. Take it slow and easy. Pat and I will stay here."

They didn't ask questions. They moved quietly, almost languidly, to their posts, while Manny and his minions watched the gambit with silent puzzlement and the man behind the gun stood tense and ready.

Nino got the anchor up. I heard the cough of the *Wahine*'s engines and the stern flurry as the gears meshed and the screw bit into the water. Then, mercifully, we were moving. Pat and I still leant against the rail and I still held the rifle tucked under my arm with the safety catch off. Manny didn't want a shooting war—yet—but if he started it, I wanted him as the first casualty.

The watchers on the rail were silent as we nosed out, still broadside to, and Johnny swung the wheel and headed eastward along the reef to the channel entrance. The man behind the gun slewed it round to follow us. Then suddenly a great roar of laughter went up. It rang like a monstrous obscenity across the clean sunlit water.

Nino, Pat and I walked aft to join Johnny Akimoto in the cockpit.

"That's the most horrible, brutal thing I've ever seen." Pat's voice was low and controlled, but her dark eyes were black with anger. "It was so cold-blooded and—and stark."

I grunted unhappily. "It was no more than I expected. The gun and the depth charges were the only surprise. But, knowing Manny, I should have been prepared for those, too."

"I think," said Nino Ferrari with judicial calm, "I think I do not like this Manny fellow very much. I think he is the son of a whore. He called me a Wop, but my people were civilized gentlemen when he was a dirty thought in his great-grandfather's mind. I shall think about him, very seriously."

Johnny Akimoto said nothing. He stood aloof at the
wheel—a dark, lonely figure, nursing the *Wahine* home-
wards with a kind of pathetic carefulness. Something had
happened to this gentle man. It was as if he and the boat
he loved had suffered a defilement from the mere
presence of the black lugger and her tatterdemalion
crew. His wise eyes were full of cold anger. The skin was
drawn tight along his cheekbones and the line of his jaw.

Not another word was spoken until we cleared the
channel and dropped anchor in the placid water of the
lagoon.

Then we held a council of war. We would transfer the
stores and the diving equipment to the beach camp. We
would move Pat's tent up the beach close to our own. We
would keep a twenty-four-hour watch on the black
lugger and her activities. We would beach the workboat
and the dinghy in sight of the camp and we would all
sleep ashore. At this point Johnny Akimoto disagreed.

"No, Renboss. You and your friends will stay ashore. I
stay with the *Wahine*."

"I don't know if that's wise, Johnny. I think we're safer
together. No harm can come to the *Wahine*. They'll see
us unloading the stores. If they decide to move in on the
island—which I doubt—they will leave her alone and
come to the camp."

Johnny shook his head. He said in a level voice, "No.
This island is your island, Renboss. The *Wahine* is my
boat. Each of us will guard what is his own. I will keep
one rifle and half the ammunition. You will take the other
gun to the camp. Nino has his pistol, so the division is
fair. Believe me, Renboss, it is better this way."

Nino Ferrari nodded agreement when I looked at
him.

"Johnny is right, my friend. Let him do as he wants.
One of us can come out each day to keep him company
and bring him fresh water. Besides, the *Wahine* is our

lifeline. She must be kept safe and in running order, in case we need her."

So it was agreed. It took us four trips in the dinghy to get all the gear ashore, and from the black lugger outside the reef Manny Mannix watched us through the long afternoon. When evening came, Nino, Pat and I sat round the campfire and saw the riding lights of the *Wahine* rise and fall on the lonely water and, farther out, the yellow glow that streamed from the cabin hatches of the big lugger.

In his detached professional voice Nino Ferrari discussed the situation.

"What happened this morning was a shameful thing, but it does not profit us to curse and sweat and be angry about it. In the end it may turn out to our advantage."

"The hell it may!" I burst out angrily. "Manny's in possession. Manny's got the equipment. Manny's got the time and the money. If we make a single move he can shoot our heads off. We've just got to sit here, and—"

A small firm hand was laid on my arm, and Pat's calm voice brought me up short.

"Let Nino finish, Renn."

Nine chuckled and winked at me.

"I told you, you got yourself a good woman, my friend. I did not tell you before, but when I saw that hold this morning, my heart was down in my flippers. I have seen these things before, you understand, and I can tell you now that more than three-quarters of that hold is buried in the sand. You saw the angle of the deck. If you will think about it you will realize that when her nose went down everything movable would slide down also. So if the chests are there they are most probably far down under the sand. There are freaks, of course, and accidents, but that is the way I read the story."

"Read it any way you like, Nino, the fact remains that Manny's got suit divers and pumps. He can work longer than we can. He can hose away the sand. He can stay out there till he does it."

Nino chuckled and shook his head.

"You amateurs! He has a pump, sure. But what sort of a pump can you work from a small crate like that? How long will it take him to shift a thousand tons of sand? You talk of time. Sure he has time, but time is money. He has the wages of the crew and the skipper and the divers. He has the charter of the boat. He will work so long, and if he does not find the treasure chests he will pack up and go home. Why? Because he is a businessman. Because there is always a limit to the amount of money he can spend. Then, when he goes, we move in. He has made our job easier for us, you see?"

Nino's logic was unshakable. I had no answer to his argument. I was an angry man. He was cool as a judge. Pat nodded her approval of his calm reasoning. I felt ashamed of my helpless anger.

Then we saw a spotlight switched on aboard the lugger. Its naked beam made a great pool of light on the water outside the reef. We heard the rattle of a winch and the steady, distant beat of a pump. We saw a monstrous shape lowered over the side of the lugger into the lighted pool.

Manny was a businessman. He knew that time was money. He was going to work round the clock.

Chapter Fifteen

We woke each morning to the steady thudding of the pumps. We saw the black lugger riding still at anchor over the wreck of the *Doña Lucia*. We saw the sleepy movement of men about her cluttered decks. We saw Johnny Akimoto perched on the bows of the *Wahine* dangling a line overside to fish for his breakfast.

We would race down to the beach to wash the sleep out of our bodies; and then, while Pat made breakfast, Nino amd I would tidy the camp and scavenge in the undergrowth for our day's supply of wood. Then one of us would take the workboat and putter out to spend the morning with Johnny aboard the *Wahine*. His anger had gone now; he was able to smile again, and he moved comfortably about the decks of the *Wahine* like a householder in his garden plot. But there was about him a quality of wariness and caution, the attitude of a man waiting for the inevitable in the midst of a brief, illusory peace.

Then, because there was nothing else to do, I would take Pat on small tours of inspection of my embattled island kingdom. I taught her the names of the trees—casuarina, tournefortia, umbrella tree, native plum. I showed her the great hoop pines, whose seeds had been carried by birds from the mainland. I showed her where the noddy terns rested under the soft leaves of the pisonias.

We picked wild orchids on the rock ledges. We sat for coolness under the drooping fronds of tree ferns. We watched the green tree-ants sewing leaves together, using their babies as a living shuttle from which came the long silky thread that bound and cemented them together. We watched them spin their stables, pens and galleries of fine silky mesh where the mealybugs lay imprisoned like domestic cattle until their time came to be killed and eaten.

We sat entranced at the angling spider who hangs from his web and fishes for fluttering moths with a drop of moist glue hung beneath his body.

We tried, and failed, to make friends with the lean and shaggy goats, protected by an old law against the needs of shipwrecked mariners. Their tracks were everywhere in the bush, and we followed them up to the saddle between the twin horns and looked down on the brown cliffs, with the white water beating at their flanks. Perched solitary, like dawn people, between the sea and the sun, Pat and I watched the glory of green islands strung on the broken strands of the reef. We saw the blue turn to green and yellow where the deeps ended and the shallows began. We saw the light slant off the heaving bodies of porpoises, and the skimming arrow-heads of flying fish, and the small dark shape of an ancient turtle that had seen, perhaps, the coming of the *Doña Lucia*.

We climbed the twin peaks and I pointed out the narrow cleft in the rocks which was the only semblance of a cave on the island. But we withdrew hurriedly from the heavy animal smell that greeted us. A bearded goat thrust his head out of the shadows and grinned at us.

Then we would go back to the camp to find Nino, stretched on the sand, sunning his dark body and grinning at us like the god of the goats himself.

Nino was a constant wonder to me. Time meant nothing to him. His spare, muscular body was endowed with a feline grace. He moved like a cat and he had the cat's capacity for instant relaxation and repose. He refused to spend his energies on profitless speculation or activity; yet his mind was clear and sharp as a knife edge.

"I am counting the days, my friend," he would say, "but I am also enjoying them. I am telling myself that, in a week—ten days—two weeks at most, they will lose heart and go away. Until then, I am enjoying myself. I have not had a holiday like this in years."

I felt an odd sense of guilt when I realized that I was thinking the same thing. Locked in the small circle of the reef, denied all opportunity for action, I had resigned myself to the calm of the lotus days and to the pastoral peace of my love for Pat Mitchell. We told ourselves that this way of life we could enjoy forever. We would build a house on the island. We would buy ourselves a boat like the *Wahine*. We would see our children grow brown and sturdy in the sun. We wove a tapestry of lovers' dreams, shot with the colours of the sunset and the sea.

Then, one day, something happened aboard the black lugger. I was watching her through the glasses when I saw a sudden flurry of movement on her decks. I heard a distant shout above the beat of the pumps. I saw the group playing cards on the forward hatch break up and scurry aft. I saw the dark body of one of the island boys scramble up from the cockpit and make as if to dive overboard. I saw him caught and held and dragged forward and flung, face down, on the hatch cover.

I saw him beaten, mightily, while the crew stood round grinning and Manny Mannix took the cigar out of his mouth and laughed and laughed.

I handed the glasses to Nino Ferrari. He stared at the scene for a moment, then passed them to Pat. She handed them back to me without a word, then walked away and retched on the sand.

The beating continued, steadily, methodically, monstrously, until the black boy had ceased to struggle and lay bloody and broken on the hatch cover.

Then I saw a horrible thing.

Manny Mannix made a curt gesture with his cigar. There was a moment's hesitation, and then four men stepped forward, took the limp form by the arms and legs and heaved it overboard. For perhaps a minute it floated, a dark mass on the smooth water, drifting slowly away with the current from the side of the lugger.

Suddenly I saw the black dorsal fin of a shark. Then another and another. There was a flurry and a threshing of water as the scavengers fought over their meal, then . . . nothing. But I thought I saw a dark stain spreading out with the ripples. I put down the glasses.

Nino Ferrari spat in the sand.

"Now," he said quietly, "now I think it is time we did something."

That evening I rowed out to the *Wahine* and brought Johnny Akimoto ashore for a discussion. He, too, had seen the terrible little drama and his eyes were smouldering with anger.

The four of us sat in the circle of firelight and watched Nino Ferrari bend forward, smooth the sand with his palm and begin to draw a map. . . .

"Here," he said, "is the island, with the beach in front and the cliffs behind. Here is the lagoon. Here is the line of the reef. Here it swings wide out in front of us. There it comes in close and becomes one with the rock shelf at the back of the island. Here is the camp. Here is the *Wahine*. And there"—he made a cross in the sand with his finger—"there is the lugger and the wreck."

He straightened up, lit his cigarette, inhaled deeply and blew out smoke from his mouth and nostrils. Then he spoke. His voice was low and even, but full of deep feeling.

"Before I tell you any more, I want to say this. A man's life is a precious thing. It is worth more than all the gold of the *Doña Lucia*, more than all the wealth in the world. I have seen many men die, some of them because of things I have done. I have seen a few men beaten and killed, as that one was killed today. In that I had no part. But the older I get, the more I know that each man's death is the death of a part of myself, because my life is sharing in theirs. I tell you this so that you will understand that what I propose is not a light thing, not a thing done for gain, but for justice."

He broke off. He smoked for a moment, silently. His eyes were veiled. The rest of us watched him, tense, expectant. Then he went on.

"I am going to blow up the lugger."

The words dropped into the silence like pebbles into a pool. Johnny Akimoto breathed out with a small sound like the hissing of a gas jet. I felt Pat stiffen. Her hands caught at my arm. She was shuddering violently. Nino Ferrari talked on calmly.

"The limpet mine is a very simple weapon. Very safe for the man who uses it. It is fixed by suction to the underside of a hull. It has a time fuse which is set to give the attacker a margin of safety in which to escape. I brought four of them with me to use on the *Doña Lucia*—now I shall use them against the lugger."

He bent forward and began again to draw in the sand, while the rest of us watched in speechless fascination.

"Here"—he pointed to a spot where the reef came close to the island under the shadow of the western horn—"here is where the current begins. It sets along the reef and runs out along the edge of it towards the spot where our friends are working. When the tide is full it makes three, perhaps four, knots. A man could enter the water here and swim down with the current. It would take him no more than half an hour to reach the ship. He would come up to it on the opposite side from that on which the divers are working. He would fix the mines and swim, still with the current, in the direction of the channel. He would shoot the channel and swim back to the *Wahine*. The whole operation would take an hour and a half—no more."

He straightened up and looked at us. His dark eyes searched our faces. It was Johnny Akimoto who spoke first.

"I think it is a good idea, Renboss. If Nino will have me, I will go with him."

Nino shook his head. "No, Johnny. This swim must be made under the water. I go alone."

Now it was my turn.

"If you go at all, Nino, I'm coming with you."

Nino looked at me. He darted a swift, warning glance towards Pat, who still clung to my arm, white and shaken. Then he said slowly, "You should understand, my friend, that in a thing like this there is always a certain risk . . . and time fuses, you understand, and the depth charges which are still lashed to the deck."

"It's my party, Nino," I said. "If you go, I go with you."

Then, sharp and high, Pat Mitchell's voice cut into our discussion.

"None of you will go. This morning we saw murder done. That's a matter for the police. We'll take the *Wahine*, or I'll take the workboat, and we'll go straight to Bowen and report what's happened here."

It was Johnny Akimoto who answered her, gravely, somberly, like a father telling a painful truth to a child.

"No, Miss Pat. The moment we try to move out of the channel, they would turn the machine gun on us. Besides"—he hesitated and then went on—"what was done this morning was done in daylight in full view. They know that we saw, and they are not frightened. Because I think—I know—that when they are ready, they have it in mind to kill us also."

To Nino and to me the logic was plain, but Pat protested it, violently.

"They couldn't, Johnny. They wouldn't dare. They couldn't hope to get away with it."

"Why not, Miss Pat? You know where we are. We are three hours' sailing from the mainland. Out there is the big ocean. I will tell you how they would do it. They would kill us first and feed our bodies to the sharks. Then they would destroy all trace of the camp. They would load the stores on the *Wahine* and tow her out into the big waters and let her drift. Then one day, perhaps, she would be washed inshore and the newspapers would call it another mystery of the sea. It would be very simple."

In the face of this stark revelation Pat was horror-stricken. She buried her face in her hands and sobbed. I put my arm round her shoulders and drew her to me to comfort her. I said gently, "I'm sorry, sweetheart, but Johnny's right. Nino's way is the only way. It's their lives or ours."

"I think," said Nino quietly, "I think maybe, the lady should go to bed. These are not pleasant matters."

"No!" The word snapped like a lash. She lifted her ravaged face, still wet with tears, and challenged us. "I will not be turned out like—like a waitress. My life is involved as yours are. I will stay and listen to what you have to say."

If I had ever loved my small tanned woman, I loved her at that moment. I was proud of her and grateful for her and humbled by the bright courage of her. I bent and kissed her while Nino grinned and Johnny Akimoto smiled his wise, slow smile of approval. Then we settled to our planning.

"It is important," said Nino Ferrari, "that there should be no moon. We have seen that each night they keep a watch on deck. The men on the pumps are busy, but this fellow walks the deck with a gun. We shall be under the water, but there are still the bubbles. If the sea is flat they are unmistakable."

Johnny Akimoto made a quick calculation.

"Tomorrow night the moon does not rise until eleven o'clock. The tide is full by eight. That will give you three hours to work."

Nino nodded and went on briskly, "Good! But it is still important that we make full use of the time." He turned to me. "Is there a place where we can get into the water without having to float ourselves across the reefs? We shall be carrying explosives, remember."

I thought for a moment, and then I remembered. Just behind the first shoulder of the western horn there was a place where the rocks dropped down into deep water, and where the sea ran in like a long tongue, into a deep cleft in the side of the island. The reef was broken at this point and, if we had strength enough to fight out twenty yards against the wash, we should strike the current that would carry us down towards the lugger. I pointed it out to Nino on the map. He questioned me meticulously. Then he was satisfied.

"So! The next thing is to plan our movements so that tomorrow will look like any other day. They watch us from the lugger, remember. They know, therefore, that Johnny stays aboard the *Wahine* and I sunbathe on the beach and you and the young lady trot about the island. Tomorrow we must do exactly the same thing. Johnny stays on the boat, one of us visits him. This time it had better be me. I can fix the mines down in the cabin. You two will take your little walk, but tomorrow it will be to the point where we are to enter the water. Then you can lead us there, quickly, when we are ready to go."

I was filled with admiration for the little Genoese. He was planning his small campaign like a great general. The stone man on the pedestal in his native town would have smiled his approval. There was one point that worried me. I put it to Nino.

"If Johnny stays on the *Wahine*, that means Pat is left here alone. I don't like that."

"Neither do I," said Nino, "but I think it is necessary. We cannot afford to make any change in our routine. She will light the fire and make the meal at the same time. She can finish her meal and go to bed, if she wants. She will have the rifle and my pistol, but I do not think she will have any need of them. On the lugger they work right through the night; besides, they will not risk her in the channel in the darkness."

Pat nodded and gave me a brave smile.

"It's all right, Renn. Really it is. I'm used to it, remember? I was alone on the island before I met you."

I submitted, of course. I had to. But I told myself that if I survived the following night I would never leave her alone again. Nino went on, patiently detailing the final stages of the operation.

"As soon as it is dark we will leave the camp. The *signorina* will have sandwiches and hot tea ready for us. We will carry them to the place where we enter the water and eat there. Better, you see, that they do not see too much movement in the camp after dark. When we enter the water, remember that we have a long swim ahead of us and we must save our strength for the swim home. Do not hurry, do not thrash about. Content yourself with keeping on course and let the current do the rest. Then, when we come to the ship, stay well under her counter, so that the bubbles will dissipate themselves out of sight of the watch. We will fix four mines . . . two amidships, the others fore and aft. I will do that myself. You will float beside me and hand me the two which you will carry. And after that . . ."

He shrugged and spread his hands in a gesture of comic resignation. For myself, I was less good-humoured about it. After that would come the half-mile race to the channel, before the mines went off and the depth charges exploded and the killing shock waves battered our tired bodies. After that, the millrace of the turbulent channel and the final swim to the *Wahine*. For most of it we would not dare surface because of the machine gun in the bows of the black lugger.

"Now," said Nino abruptly, "we go to bed. And you, young lady"—he thrust a bony finger at Pat and grinned like the father of all the goats—"you go to bed first. Kiss your man and tell him you love him. Then go to bed. Love is a tiring business, and tomorrow he will be swimming for his life."

She laughed and kissed me and clung to me a brief moment. Then she walked to her tent, a brave small figure, shoulders squared, head high.

When she was out of earshot Nino turned to me. He wasn't grinning now. He was dead serious. He said bluntly, "I made it sound as simple as I could for the lady. But it is not simple. We are swimming in bad waters to the limit of our air supply. By midnight tomorrow night we may both be dead. Understand that."

"I understand, Nino."

He turned to Johnny Akimoto. He spoke tersely, crisply, a general giving the last battle orders to his staff.

"Johnny, this is an operation that runs to time. If it does not, it fails, and we are dead men. We should be back by ten o'clock. That is the extreme limit of the air supply. Give us till eleven. If we are not aboard then, you will know that we are dead."

Johnny nodded gravely. Nino continued.

"What you will not know is whether we have managed to fix the mines or not. So this is what you will do. You will take the dinghy and row inshore as quietly as you can and pick up the girl and bring her out to the *Wahine*. Then you will start the engines and head out through the channel at full speed. You will have a little start, because they will have to get the men up from the bottom of the sea and that takes time. After that they will come for you, shooting. You understand?"

"I understand very well," said Johnny.

I understood, too. In his dry, crackling, professional voice Nino had been discussing our funeral arrangements.

Chapter Sixteen

Johnny was going back to the *Wahine*. I walked with him
down to the beach and stood with him on the damp sand
under the bright, cold stars. Each of us knew that this
might be our last meeting.

"Look after my girl, Johnny," I said.

"With my life, Renboss," said Johnny Akimoto.

I told him about the money in the bank on the
mainland. I told him how, if anything happened to me,
the money would be paid to him. He shook his head.

"No, Renboss. Not to me. You have your own wahine
to look after."

"She doesn't need it, Johnny. She wouldn't take it
anyway. I want you to have it."

"Thank you, Renboss," said Johnny.

It takes a great gentleman to accept a gift gracefully.
Johnny Akimoto was a very great gentleman. I thanked
him—banally enough, God knows—for all he had done
for me. I tried, with halting, awkward phrases, to convey
all that I had come to feel for him: respect, admiration,
the kind of love that grows between men who have
drunk the wine of triumph together and tasted the stale,
sour lees of defeat.

He heard me out with embarrassment. Then, quite
simply, he said a strange and beautiful thing which I shall
remember till the day I die.

"Wherever you are, Renboss, my heart will be with you. Wherever I am, your heart will be with me. Good night . . . my brother."

Then he took my hand and pressed it to his naked breast, released it and was gone. I heard the rattle of the oarlocks and the ripple and dip of the oars as he sculled back to the *Wahine*. God has made few men like Johnny Akimoto. I have often wondered if he made all of them black.

The next day began like all the other days.

We swam before breakfast. We pottered about the camp. And when the chores were done, Nino took the workboat and went out to the *Wahine*. He carried with him a small wooden box in which were the limpet mines and the detonators, packed in cotton wool. Pat and I strolled out, hand in hand, to explore the tracks that led to our launching place. The whole island was crossed and recrossed with goat pads, but we needed a path that we could follow without difficulty in the darkness and which would be screened from the beach and the watchman on the black lugger.

We found it without difficulty. We calculated that Nino and I could walk it comfortably in fifteen minutes. We climbed down to the launching place and studied it carefully, noting the juts and hollows in the rocks and the snags that would be hidden by the high water. Then we retraced our steps, checking the landmarks that would guide us in the darkness—a twisted tree trunk, a jutting rock, a clump of tree ferns, the perfumed blossoms of a solitary ginger flower.

Then, our survey completed, we made our way through the bush to the small valley with the grassy bank and the drooping of rock lilies. The shade was grateful to us, and the cool was kind. The words we spoke were simple, private, pitiful. We were a man and woman who loved each other and who knew that the next twelve hours might see the end of all love and the death of all desire. Yet we were like the old, old lovers turned to marble in the market square whose hands are clasped, whose eyes look always into each other's but whose lips are parted a hair's breadth from a kiss and whose bodies ache eternally for ecstasies that will never come.

Nino Ferrari was right—love is an expensive luxury when a man must swim for his life.

We turned our backs on our disappointed paradise and walked out of the bush into the sun.

Nino was in his usual place on the beach. This time he was not sunbathing. He was sitting propped against a small mound of sand, scanning the black lugger through the field glasses. When we came to him, he grunted a greeting, told us with a curt gesture to sit beside him and continued his scrutiny of the boat. Then he handed the glasses to me. He was frowning.

"Tell me what you make of that, my friend."

It was a curious and puzzling little scene. One of the divers was sitting in the midst of a small ring of spectators with a square, dark object at his feet. His helmet had been unscrewed and was lying on the deck beside him, but the rubberized fabric of his suit was shining and dripping with water. He had evidently just come up. He was pointing to the dark object and gesticulating awkwardly as if explaining where and how he had found it.

The crew were grouped round him in a broken circle. Manny Mannix stood facing the diver. I could not see his face, but I caught the familiar flourish of the cigar. I knew that he was questioning the diver closely.

"Well, my friend, what is it all about, do you think?"

I lowered the glasses and turned to Nino.

"I don't know exactly. On the face of it, the diver's brought up something from the wreck and they're just standing round discussing it."

"You know what it is they have brought up?"

"No. It's dark and squarish—that's all I know. Every time I tried to get a better look, some fool shifted his feet and I couldn't focus on it."

"I saw it," said Nino soberly. "It is our box. The one we found in the cabin."

I burst out laughing. The thought of Manny Mannix, frustrated and fuming over that empty sea-rotten box, was too much for me. I threw back my head and roared.

"I'm glad you think it's funny, my friend."

Nino's icy voice was like water thrown in my face. I stopped laughing and looked at him. Then I looked at Pat. Her face was as troubled as Nino's.

"I don't get it," I said. "I'm sorry to be so dull, but I don't get it. Maybe I have a peculiar sense of humour, but I think that's very funny . . . funny, indeed."

"No," said Nino tersely, trenchantly. "Not funny. Not funny at all. Very unfortunate for all of us. They have found our box. They have been working for many days now, with divers and pumping equipment. They have found nothing but that single broken box. Now they are telling themselves that perhaps we have found the treasure and carried it ashore. They are telling themselves that is why we did not put up a fight, but let ourselves be pushed off the diving area without so much as a dirty word. Soon, I think, very soon, they will come in to take us."

I was horror-struck. The stark simplicity of the situation, the sudden wreck of all our careful plans, left me for a moment without power of thought or speech. I looked out towards the *Wahine* and saw that Johnny Akimoto was standing in the bows, shading his eyes with his hand, watching the men on the deck of the lugger. I wondered if his thoughts were the same as ours.

I raised the glasses again. I saw the circle of men break up. I saw them moving about the decks with the disciplined hurry of those turning to an urgent but familiar task. I saw the pump hands stripping the diver of his heavy suit. I saw the winch man winding in his cable, making it fast on the drum and throwing the canvas cover over it. I handed the glasses to Nino.

"You're right, Nino. They're making ready to move."

"Then," said Nino curtly, "it is time for us to move also."

I pointed to the *Wahine*.

"What about Johnny?"

"Johnny knows what is going on as well as we do. We cannot help him, he cannot help us. If he wants to join us he has time to do so, but I do not think he will leave the *Wahine*."

"Nino's right, Renn," said Pat quietly.

"But they'll kill him!"

"I think," said Nino dryly, "they will try to kill all of us. Johnny has the rifle and ammunition. He has the same chance as we have—a slightly better one, I think, unless they try to board him, which I doubt they will do."

There was a moment's silence. We watched them get the anchor up. We heard them start the engines. We saw the flurry of water under the stern of the lugger. Then they were moving.

"Come," said Nino briskly. "Back to the camp. There is work to do."

We turned and went up to the camp at a run. We arrived panting and breathless, but Nino would brook no delay. His voice crackled in a running fire of orders.

"We have twenty minutes, perhaps half an hour. No more. They have not run the channel before. They will take it carefully. They will go to the *Wahine*. After that they will come for us. Sooner or later you will have to stand and fight. Is there a place where you can do that?"

I tried to marshal my thoughts. They were like sheep, scattered by fright on a country road. It was Pat who answered for me. Her voice was cool and controlled.

"The western horn. The cleft in the rock. It goes in a long way. It is in the angle between the main saddle and the shoulder that falls down to the sea. That's only one way to reach it. They must come up the goat track. With a rifle we can hold them off a long time."

Nino grinned sourly.

"Didn't I say you'd got yourself a good woman? Now, listen, and listen carefully. You will take a water bag and food. You will take the rifle and the ammunition. You will take the knife from your diving belt in case . . . in case the ammunition runs out, or you have to fight quietly in the bush, then the two of you will make your way up to the cleft in the rock. Is that clear?"

"Quiet clear, but what about you? Aren't you coming with us?"

"No, but what I will do concerns you as well, so you must understand clearly what I am telling you. They cannot run the lugger inshore. So they will send a party to the beach in a boat. They will be armed. They will search the camp first. Then they will beat the island, looking for you."

I nodded agreement.

Nino talked on crisply. "When you are gone, with the *signorina*, I will take the lung pack and the pistol and two of the limpet mines, which is all I can carry. I will go through the bush and find a place where I can hide myself in the rocks and enter the water without being seen. Then, when I can, I will enter the water and swim out to the lugger and fix the mines. I will set them on a three-hour fuse, then I will swim to the *Wahine* and float myself under her blind side until I have a chance to get myself aboard. That is my party. This is yours."

He paused and wiped the sweat from his face with the back of his hand. Pat and I watched him silently, full of admiration for this small dark fellow with the icy courage and the brain like an adding machine.

He continued. "You will go up to the cleft in the rock under the western horn. Soon—in an hour, ninety minutes—they will come up for you. You will have to pin them down with rifle fire so that they do not move out of the bushes. Then—I cannot think how, but you will know—you will have to work your way out of the rock hole into the bush and down again to the beach. Then you will swim to the *Wahine*. If God wills, I shall be waiting for you. We shall run her out through the channel before the big blowup. Is it clear now?"

It was as clear as water. Our small force would be broken up—Johnny on the *Wahine*, Nino keeping his solitary vigil behind the rocks, Pat and I penned in our hole in the hill waiting for the chance to slip through the bush like hunted beasts and make our way down to the water. There was nothing to add, nothing to subtract, the tally was made. It was time to go. I stretched out my hand, Nino took it.

"Good luck, Nino!"

"Good luck, my friend—and to the little lady!"

Pat took his small lean face in her hands and kissed him.

"Thanks, Nino. God keep you."

I slung the field glasses round my neck and hooked a small flashlight to my belt. We picked up the rifle and the ammunition and the water bag and a small package of food and walked off into the bush. Nino stood a moment looking out across the water, then he turned away and went into the tent.

Halfway up the hill we stopped and looked back. A break in the trees gave us a clear view of the lagoon and the outer reef.

The black lugger was coming through the channel now. We saw her buck a little in the troubled water, then slide forward into the calm. They cut the engines and she moved slowly forward towards the anchorage of the *Wahine*. She was about three cable lengths away when they dropped the hook. I swore softly. The boys knew their business. They were moored slap across the channel. The *Wahine* could not get out without a wide detour through which the machine gun could rake every inch of her decks. We saw a boat lowered and half a dozen men climb into her. There were four at the oars and one in the stern with a rifle on his knees. There was another in the bows.

We looked at the *Wahine*. Johnny Akimoto was standing amidships, a little back from the rail, the rifle trailing easily below his hip. The rowers rowed the boat with long, easy strokes across the intervening water, until they were almost under the counter of the *Wahine*. Then they backed water and held her, rocking a little against the wash. Johnny Akimoto did not move.

I glanced back at the black lugger. Manny Mannix and the rest of the crew lined the deck. There was a man behind the machine gun in the bows. He was squatting and sighting it across the decks of the *Wahine*.

When I shifted the glasses back to her I saw that Johnny was still standing in the same position, while the fellow in the bows of the rowboat was talking and waving his hands. He wanted to come aboard. Johnny shook his head. The fellow talked again; his gestures were jerky, like those of an angry puppet. I saw Johnny raise the rifle slowly, ever so slowly. I caught the movement of his hand as he shoved the bolt home and threw off the safety catch.

Then a burst from the machine gun cut him down.

Chapter Seventeen

The sea birds rose in screaming horror from the rocks and from the reefs. The echoes of the shots rang shatteringly along the ridge between the peaks. In one suspended moment of shock and terror we saw the body of Johnny Akimoto flung backwards into the air, fall, twitching and jerking, against the cabin hatch, and then lie still.

Pat buried her face in her hands. Her body was shaken by deep, shuddering sobs. The echoes died. The sea birds settled again, and the silence of death hung in the bright air between the island and the sea.

Then my belly knotted and I vomited on the dead leaves. When I looked up again I saw that the men from the dinghy were scurrying over the ship like rats— diving down the companionway, ripping off the hatch covers, defiling every corner of the boat which had been Johnny Akimoto's woman. Then anger rose in me, deep, soul-wrenching agony, that set me gibbering obscenities and leaping and shouting like a madman at the men who had killed my brother. Then the anger died to blank wretchedness and we turned away, climbing slowly up the hill and along the saddle to the dark cleft in the rocks.

A stale animal smell hung heavily about the entrance. When I shone the flashlight inside, an aged goat bleated and shot out between our feet. His hair was long and matted and he stank foully. The floor inside was deep in his droppings. I shone the light on the rear wall and saw that it was broken by another narrower cleft beyond which was blackness. When I flashed the beam on the roof, a small colony of bats stirred and squeaked and made a small panic, then settled again as I shone the light round the walls.

Pat shivered and drew close to me. The flashlight pried out a small angle in the rock walls. I scraped the filth away with the sole of my shoe and set down the food and the water bag and the clips of ammunition. I turned to Pat and pointed.

"When the shooting starts, sweetheart, that's where you'll be—head down and tucked well behind the angle of the rock. It's not much help, when they start shooting into the cave and the slugs start whipping off the walls, but at least you'll be able to pass the spare clips to me."

She nodded, as if she could not trust herself to speak. I took her hand and drew her out into the sunlight. In the bushes near the cave we found two large rocks, covered with moss. These we carried and set across the entrance so that they made a small crenellation that would give me some small protection when the shooting started and leave me a reasonable traverse of the path below.

We scouted the bush on either side of the cleft, noting with desperate precision every bush and rock and fallen log that might shield us when we made our desperate dash down to the beach. I clutched at the small consolation when I saw how steeply the goat track fell away in front of the cleft and how a man approaching it from below must walk straight into my sights.

Then, our survey made, our small fortress prepared as much as it could ever be against the coming siege, we stood together in front of the dark hole in the rock and looked down to the camp and the beach and the sea.

The rats had left the *Wahine* now. They had nosed and

scampered and pried and then gone overside, their
appetites unsatisfied. The dasrk, crumpled figure still lay
against the cabin hatch, and the *Wahine* rocked in the
water, like a woman nursing her lonely grief.

Now they were coming ashore—two boatloads of them
this time—four men to a boat, with Manny Mannix
sitting in the stern of the leading craft. The sunlight
glistened on their sweating backs as they bent to the
oars, and I saw their lips move in talk and laughter,
though I could not hear a sound. They were armed—two
with automatic rifles, the rest with pistols and standard
.303s. They drove hard inshore and beached the boats
high up on the sand. Then they spread out and advanced
up the slope towards the camp, with Manny Mannix
bringing up the rear, like the cautious fellow he was.

The noise of their shouting drifted up faintly, as we
watched them scrambling about the camp, upending
crates and boxes, ripping the tops off them, kicking them
aside with angry disappointment. Then, when they
found nothing, they stopped. They gathered round
Manny and stood dejectedly while he harangued them.
We could guess what he was telling them. The treasure
must be on the island somewhere. If they found us they
would find it, too. We saw him point upwards to the
ridge, making a long sweep with his arm in the direction
of the upper slopes. We saw him bend down and trace
lines in the sand while the others bowed their heads to
look at him. Then he straightened up. The men strung
themselves out in a long line on the tussocky fringe of
the sand. Manny took his place in the center of the line.
I saw him put his hand into the breast of his white coat
and withdraw it, holding a long-barrelled black pistol.
Then he waved and shouted something which I could
not hear, and the whole line moved slowly forward into
the bush.

They were coming after us. It was time to retire to our
fortress in the rock.

When we were inside, I made Pat lie down on her stomach on the floor, so that her head was protected by the skirt of the rock. I was worried about what might happen when Manny and his boys began shooting into the cave mouth. The bullets would go buzzing like angry bees, ricocheting between the walls. A sudden thought occurred to me.

I handed her the flashlight, warning her to shield the light with her hand, and sent her back to explore the narrow opening in the rear wall. She started to protest. I silenced her with a gesture. I heard her move gingerly into the darkness. I saw the small reddish glow of the light shining through her fingers. Then she called softly.

"It's quite large, Renn. I can't see all of it. But there's quite a big wall to the left of the entrance. The floor's clean, too."

"Good! Lie down behind it. Switch off the light. And don't come out, whatever happens. If anything happens to me, stay there. There's just a chance that they'll think I'm alone and leave you there."

I heard her give a small cry and I half turned to comfort her. Then, quite near, I heard voices and the crashing of clumsy men through the bush.

I called softly, warning her. She did not answer.

I took a long swig from the water bag, drew the clips of ammunition close to my hand and sprawled in the firing position between the two stones.

I worked the bolt of the rifle and then shot it home, shoving a shell into the breech. Then I thrust the barrel out between the rocks, enough to give me a traverse of the approach, laid the butt of it hard against my shoulder and sighted down the sloping path.

That was the way they would come. There was no other approach. They might strike down from the ridge, they might move upwards along the flank of the hill, but at the end they must come out on the goat track and I would see them.

I tried to think what I would do if I were planning Manny's tactics for him. I told myself that I would set two men with automatic rifles in the bushes on either side of the track. These two would begin pouring crossfire into the cave, enfilading me, pinning me down, while the others crept up along the bush fringe to jump me at point-blank range. One man, with a single-action rifle, could not long survive a maneuver like that. I took small courage from the thought that Manny had fought his war from King's Cross and might well have forgotten what they had taught him as a rookie.

My body was cramped; my arms ached. My elbows were frayed by the rough floor. The sweat was pouring down my face; the small nodule of the foresight wavered and trembled. I shifted and eased myself a little as the noise came closer.

They had lost formation now. Their voices were scattered. They stumbled and cursed and shouted to one another when they lost contact among the tree trunks and the thick bushes and the trailing vines. I pictured them, sweating and angry, their flesh torn by brambles and twigs, tormented by flies and buzzing gnats, and I smiled sourly to myself.

Then they seemed to come together. The footsteps converged on a spot near the bottom of the track. The shouting ceased. There was a babble of voices, then a murmur, over which I heard a single harsh voice crackling in a spate of unintelligible words. Then the murmuring began again—sullen, protesting.

Three seconds later Manny Mannix stepped out on the track. His white duck suit was crumpled and stained. He had lost his hat. His face was streaked with sweat and grime. He looked angry and unhappy. His mouth was working; I heard the nasal, snarling sound of his voice, but I could not distinguish the words. He waved his pistol dangerously and pointed first at the ground, then, with a wide sweep, at the surrounding bush. Then he raised his head and stared straight into the mouth of the cave.

I shot him between the eyes.

The impact carried him backwards down the path, spinning. He crumpled and lay still.

I heard the shot echo along the ridge. I heard the sudden riot of the sea birds. I ejected the spent shell and shoved another up the spout. Now, I thought, they would come.

But they didn't come. They broke and ran.

I heard a voice scream: "Manny's had it!"

Then the whole sorry crew ran, stumbling and plunging and yelling down the slope. Then I was standing in the mouth of the cave firing wildly into the bush. I heard a yelp of pain and the crash of a falling body and I shouted and fired again and again, laughing crazily as I heard the high whine of the bullets through the trees. . . .

I wondered, irrelevantly, what had happened to Nino Ferrari.

Then Pat was beside me and we stood together watching the wild stampede break through the fringe of the bush and stumble drunkenly down to the waiting boats. I flung the hot rifle on the ground and propped myself against the rock face, sobbing and retching and trembling like a man with fever.

When the spasm had passed, Pat handed me the water bag and I drank, gagging at first, then gulping down the cool, flat liquid as if there were a fire in my belly. Then I upended it and poured the water over my face and neck and breast as if to wash away the slime of a nightmare that had clung to me even after waking. Her control broke, too, and she sobbed and clung to me, her face against my breast, kissed me, clinging to me, weeping and laughing at once, pressing my body to hers as if to assure herself that it was still living and whole . . . not lying as Manny's lay, a bloodied wreck on the goat path, with the flies buzzing round its ravaged face.

She took me by the hand and led me back into the cave.

I was too weary to question her, too spent to puzzle on small mysteries. Meekly I let myself be led across the filthy floor of the first chamber to the dark opening in the wall. Pat switched on the flashlight.

I saw a large vaulted chamber, three times as large as the first, with a sandy floor and walls of ironstone down which the water seeped slowly over a coating of green fungoid growths.

She swung the beam of the flashlight until it came to rest in the far corner. She said softly, "Look, Renn!"

I started back in momentary terror. Stretched on the sandy floor were the bleached bones of a skeleton. Two paces away was another, face downwards . . . its flesh-less fingers clutched the sand. Its knees were drawn up under its ribs in a fetal attitude.

Pat's hand was trembling. The flashlight wavered on the weird latticework of naked bones. I took the flashlight from her and gripped it firmly. We moved closer.

The first skeleton was lying on its back. The bones were slightly displaced by the nuzzling of the goats which had stripped it of every shred of clothing that had not rotted and crumbled with the passing of the centuries. Just beyond the reach of its fingers was an ancient pistol. Its wooden stock was mouldy and worm-eaten, and the metal was rusted beyond repair.

Round the little finger of the skeleton was a loose gold band in which a large cabochon ruby glowed dully under the dust of centuries. But this was not all.

Through the naked trellis of the ribs a long, thin knife had been driven, so that its rusted blade still stuck deep in the sand. The steel was pitted and corroded, but the hilt was crusted with jewels that winked and glowed under the beam of the torch.

"He was murdered," said Pat quietly.

I nodded and turned the beam on the other skeleton. The fingers were buried deep in the sand into which they had clawed in their last struggle for life. The face of the skull was buried, too, but the back of it was exposed—a smooth yellow spheroid of bone, pierced by a large round hole.

"He stabbed the other fellow," I said. "Then he was shot as he turned away."

"Yes. But there's something else, Renn. Look!"

I focussed the light and bent closer to the sand.

Clearly visible through the bleached ribs of the skeleton, clutched against his breastbone, as he must have clutched them in the last brief agony, was a pile of gold coins.

We had found the treasure of the *Doña Lucia*.

Pat caught at my arm. She was trembling violently, but she forced herself to speak.

"They escaped, Renn. Don't you see? They escaped the wreck in which all their shipmates died. They struggled ashore with these small remnants of a fortune—the jewelled dagger and the bag of gold coins." Her voice rose higher with the first onset of hysteria. "They were fortunate. They had been granted mercy. But they didn't value it. All they valued was this. . . ."

"Steady, sweetheart! Steady!" I put my arm about her shoulders to comfort her. "It was all a long, long time ago. It was done and finished two hundred years ago."

She pushed herself free and hammered at my chest with small fists. Her voice was an anguished cry.

"It didn't finish! It never finishes! It happens all the time. Men fighting and killing each other for this—this yellow refuse that even the goats reject. It happened today, Renn. It happened to you and me and Nino, and Johnny Akimoto."

Then it was as if she had been struck in the face. The wild light was quenched in her eyes. Her mouth dropped slackly. She stared at me in blank misery.

"Johnny's dead, Renn . . . Johnny Akimoto's dead. . . ."

She crumpled and I caught her in my arms and carried her like a sick child into the sun.

Chapter Eighteen

I laid her down on a bed of leaves in the shade of a big pisonia tree. I ripped off my shirt and folded it under her head. I bathed her face and forced a little of the water between her lips. After a few moments she opened her eyes and stared at me blankly; then her head lolled slackly to one side and she lapsed into the deep sleep of utter exhaustion.

I stood for a moment looking down at her, touched with weary desire for this small perfect body and with pity and love and gratitude for the bright, brave spirit which it covered. Then I left her sleeping and walked the few paces back to the mouth of the cave.

Soon we would have a long walk and a long swim ahead of us, and my tired dark girl was in no condition to face them yet. I looked down at the lagoon and saw that the boats had come alongside the black lugger and their crew were being hauled aboard by the deckwatch. The *Wahine* was still riding at anchor. The body of Johnny Akimoto still lay untended on the sweltering deck. There was no sign of Nino Ferrari.

I sat down on a slab of brown rock, lit a cigarette and considered the situation.

Manny's small army of scalawags had broken and run at the first shot; but there was no guarantee that they might not regret their cowardice and come again, better

led, to make another search for us and for the treasure.
Even so, we could not leave the island until they came
ashore again. We would have to make a surface swim to
the *Wahine*, right under the muzzle of the machine gun.

On the other hand, if they delayed too long the limpet
bombs would go off and the depth charges would
explode when the lugger sank. The *Wahine* was moored
so close to her that she could not possibly escape
damage, even total wreck. Unmanned, she might easily
be wrenched from her moorings and flung onto the reef
by the first waves from the explosion.

If that happened we might be in a worse situation than
before—killers and victims alike marooned on a barrier
island. I shivered in the warm sun. The prospect was
grotesque but very possible. Three hours, Nino had
said. Three hours from the time he fixed the mines to the
hull of the black lugger. I thought that not more than an
hour and a half had passed since Pat and I had left the
beach for the hill. Allowing time for Nino's swim, I
thought there were not more than two hours to the
blowup.

I scanned the green water of the lagoon for any sign of
Nino's shadow in the refracted sunlight. There was no
shadow. There was no flicker or ripple that could show
where he was.

I looked over at the lugger. The crew were huddled in
a shouting, gesticulating group amidships. They were
arguing, accusing each other. They were discussing the
merit of another foray for the treasure, or a quick run up
the reef and into safe waters before news of the killing
reached the mainland. There are a hundred islands
between Macasar and Bandung where a man with a boat
and a willing crew can name his own price for a little
honest gun-running.

I noticed that the boats were still tied alongside, their
oars inboard, their bows bobbing and thumping against
the planks. I thought that if they did not get the boats

inboard in twenty minutes they would mean to stay and
search for us in their own time. If they hauled them
inboard and lashed them, they would be leaving very
soon. If they were not gone within two hours, the lugger
would blow up inside the reef and there would be bloody
murder done on the white sand of my island.

I decided that I would let Pat sleep a little longer; then
we would go down to the beach and wait. If the lugger
left, well and good. If she stayed, we would wait till after
the explosion, then take the workboat and head for the
mainland.

I realized with a start that I had no means of warning
Nino Ferrari. I had no way of letting him know that we
were even alive. Even if, half submerged under the
counter of the *Wahine*, he had seen the wild rush to the
shore, it could have meant any one of half a dozen things
to him.

Then an idea occurred to me. Allow twenty minutes
more for Pat to be rested enough for the walk back to the
beach. Allow half an hour for the walk. There would still
be an hour before the mines went off. Time enough for
me to don my own diving gear and swim out across the
lagoon to the *Wahine*. There was the problem of
entering the water without being seen from the lugger.
But Nino had done it; so could I.

Now that the decision was made, I felt suddenly weary
and vaguely resentful of the new demand for effort and
strength. I looked at Pat. She was still sleeping. Her
breathing was deep and regular and the colour was
flowing slowly back under the ivory skin. A small insect
lighted on her face; she stirred uneasily and brushed it
off with an instinctive gesture, but did not waken.

As I sat there, slack and tired, and saw my girl
sleeping and all the green wonder of the island spread
below me, and all the blue stretch of ocean running out
to the rim of the world, I was conscious of a feeling new
and strange to me. A sense of truncation and of loss,

because my friend was dead and because the last shreds of innocence had been ripped away when I had seen the naked evil of the world and when I had killed the man who most of all embodied it. I felt no guilt, only distaste and disillusion. But I felt something else, too—a sense of possession and of permanence, as if I, the landless man, were now free of his own possession, as if I, the blind historian, had opened my eyes at last to see the wild wonder of the world and to know that I, too, was part of its turbulent history.

A man is fully grown when he has learnt this truth: There is no mercy in the world, except the mercy of the Almighty. There is neither peace nor permanence nor secure possession until a man straddles his small standing place and dares all comers to thrust him out of it.

I stood up, trod out my cigarette and walked back to the cave. I picked up the empty water bag, ripped open the top seam of the canvas and carried it into the big vaulted chamber. I turned over the huddled skeleton, surprised to find there was so little weight in it, and scooped the tarnished coins into the water bag. They filled it almost to the top. Then I put my hand on the jewelled hilt of the dagger and drew it out of the sand and put it on top of the coins.

The coins did not burn me. The dagger did not cut my hand.

Men had died because of them. I had fought and survived to enjoy them. They were mine to use or misuse as I pleased.

I straightened and stood a moment looking down at the pitiful bleached relics on the sand. They had nothing to say to me, nor I to them. The gulf of two centuries lay between us and their voices were blown away long since by the desert winds of time.

I snapped off the flashlight, picked up the water bag and walked out of the cave.

I wakened Pat and lifted her to her feet. She gave me a

wan little smile and said, "I'm sorry, Renn. It wasn't very thoughtful of me, was it?"

I kissed her and held her to me for a moment. Then I told her what we were going to do. I handed her the glasses and showed her the deck of the lugger, where the shouting men were quiet now, squatting in a small circle round the skipper, discussing the next move. The boats were still in the water, bobbing. She handed the glasses back to me.

"Renn?"

"Yes, sweetheart?"

"Do you think Nino's still alive?"

"Of course. We can't see him because he's probably still in the water. He'd be floating under the counter of the *Wahine*, saving the last of his air for the swim home. Nino's done this sort of thing before, remember?"

She nodded and said softly, "Renn, I wish it were all over."

"It will be, sweetheart," I told her gravely. "It'll all be over before sunset."

I stuffed the remaining clips of ammunition into my pocket, gave her the small parcel of food, then picked up the rifle and bent down for the water bag that held the last of the *Doña Lucia*'s treasure. When Pat saw it, she looked at me oddly but said nothing. I answered her unspoken question.

"Yes, sweetheart, I'm taking it. I'm taking it because we fought for it and we've won it. I'm taking it because there are debts to pay and a house and a life to build for both of us."

She shivered a little and said, "There's blood on it, Renn."

"Yes, there is blood on it, sweetheart. There's blood on the island, too. There's blood on the decks of the *Wahine*. There's blood on every acre and every doorstep where men have come, first in peace, and then have fought against those who have come, in violence, to destroy their peace. Do you understand?"

"Give me time, Renn," she pleaded quietly. "Give me time and a little love. Then I will understand."

We walked down the goat path where the body of Manny Mannix lay festering in the sun. We stepped over it and, without a backward glance, turned downwards through the trees.

When we came to the last fringe of bush before the camp we dropped to the ground and pushed aside the leaves, looking out across the water towards the black lugger. One of the boats was already inboard. Two men were lashing it to its place on the deck. The other was just being hauled up.

They were going away.

For long minutes we lay there, hardly daring to hope.

Then we saw the anchor pulled up and we heard the engines start. Slowly the black lugger nosed out towards the channel. We stood up and walked into the camp.

Nino Ferrari was lying on the warm sand, smoking a cigarette.

"I thought you would come," he said blandly.

The sublime effrontery of the man took my breath away.

"What the devil . . ."

He waved a slim brown hand.

"I made better time than I hoped. I fixed the charges, then I swam over to the *Wahine* for a breather. I heard one shot, then when I saw them running like cattle onto the beach, I guessed what had happened."

"I killed Manny Mannix."

"I know. I waited until they rowed out to the lugger. Then, while they were busy explaining what heroes they had been, I swam back to shore. I was tired. I needed a rest."

Then I showed him the water bag with the gold coins and the dagger.

He whistled softly.

"Where?"

"In the cave, behind the cleft. Pat found them . . . with two skeletons. They had killed each other."

"They always do in the end," said Nino flatly.

Then I saw that there was no laughter in his eyes. His face was grey. He looked tired and rather old. In the same flat voice he answered the question I dared not put to him.

"Very soon now."

He heaved himself up from the sand and the three of us walked down to the water's edge.

The tide was running in strongly, and the black lugger was butting her way out through the channel. The men on her decks were looking back towards the island and pointing. The thought came to me that perhaps they intended to work the wreck again, or that, having seen us, they would put about when they had cleared the channel and return to the attack.

But they did not. The lugger thrust out of the rip and into the wide water. The man at the wheel held her firmly on a southward course until she was out of the reef current, then he turned her eastward and the westering sun threw long shadows from her spars across the water.

Then it happened.

We heard the dull boom of an explosion, then another. Great spouts of water were flung into the air. The lugger seemed to heave itself up until we saw the line of her keelson. Then she settled again with a great gushing splash, heeling over as she hit the water. We saw the bodies of men flung, like dolls, high into the air to fall back into the boiling sea. Then she rolled clean over. Her spars dipped and her hatches were covered and we saw the gaping holes that had been blown in her timbers. Then the waters closed over her, heaving and bubbling and churning, while the bodies of the crew

were tossed about like corks and scraps of wreckage were
flung like chips in the maelstrom.

We saw the waters subside slowly and great waves
spread out and come racing towards the reef. Some of
the men were clinging to pieces of wreckage; others lay
in the rocking waters as if dead. Two or three were
striking out with pitiful slowness towards the island.

"It is not finished yet," said Nino Ferrari.

Seconds passed—long, inexorable seconds—while the
three of us stood in silent horror at the water's edge.
Then, one after another, the depth charges went off
. . . four of them.

Again there was the leaping and spouting of water and
the spilling of bodies, like drops from a fountain, back
into the sea. Sand and fish and weed were vomited
upwards from the ocean bed. The water spewed and
bubbled like pools of volcanic mud.

There were no swimmers now, only bobbing, helpless
shapes in a waste of wild water. For hours it seemed—
though it could not have been more than ten minutes—
we stood like stone figures, looking out on the last,
horrifying act of an ancient, bloody tragedy.

Then the bubbling and the heaving subsided and the
long waves spread out. The westering sun splashed gold
and crimson on the open water. We saw the black fins of
the sharks converging on the kill.

Pat Mitchell and I turned and walked slowly up the
beach towards the tent.

When I looked back I saw that Nino Ferrari was still
standing, a lean, pitiless figure, at the water's edge. His
back was straight. His head was unbowed. He shaded his
eyes with his hand and stared out across the blood-red
water.

His long, distorted shadow lay beside him . . . like a
gallows on the sand.

Epilogue

Between the circling arms of the island a house has been built. From its deep, shadowy veranda you look out across the lagoon to where the *Wahine* rides at anchor. There is a trailing of white trumpet flowers and a crimson burst of bougainvillaea.

There is a small browned smiling woman and a toddling boy who come down the coral path to the beach and wave me in from the channel, and wait for me while I drop the hook and loose the dinghy and scull home at the end of an island run.

We walk up the path, hand in hand, until we come to the small plot with its border of branched coral and its square white headstone. We stop. I pluck a scarlet hibiscus bloom and drop it in front of the stone, while the boy watches, fascinated, the familiar ritual.

The flower will wilt soon in the sun, but there will always be another and another, so long as we live on our Island of the Twin Horns. When my son is older, I will teach him the meaning of the plot and the cemetery, and the words which are cut into the headstone. . . .

In Memory
Of a Great and Courageous Gentleman
JOHNNY AKIMOTO
This Is His Island.
We, His Friends, Hold It in Trust for Him.
REQUIESCAT.

ABOUT THE AUTHOR

MORRIS WEST, a native Australian, was born in Melbourne in 1916. When he was fourteen he began studying as a postulant with the Christian Brothers order but left twelve years later without having taken final vows. After serving with Australian Army Intelligence during World War II, he became a partner in a flourishing recording and transcription business but left it when he discovered that he preferred to write for himself rather than for sponsors.

A stay in Italy resulted in his book *Children of the Sun*, a study of street urchins, which became an English best seller in 1957. There followed two novels published in the United States under the titles *The Crooked Road* and *Backlash*, in 1957 and 1958 respectively.

In 1958, also, Mr. West returned to Italy as Vatican correspondent for *The Daily Mail*, and he then absorbed much of the technical background for a new novel. *The Devil's Advocate*, published in 1959, promptly became that rare phenomenon in publishing—a book universally hailed by critics as a major creative work while selling, in various editions, more than two million copies. Mr. West followed it with more major successes: *Daughter of Silence* (1962), *The Shoes of the Fisherman* (1963), *The Ambassador* (1965), and *The Tower of Babel* (1967). He is also the author of *Harlequin*, *Proteus*, and *The Clowns of God*.

Mr. West has lived in England and Italy, and presently lives in New South Wales, Australia.

MORRIS WEST

If you liked this Morris West favorite, you'll want all these thrilling bestsellers.

☐	24248	GALLOWS ON THE SAND	$3.50
☐	23713	THE NAKED COUNTRY	$2.95
☐	23483	THE CROOKED ROAD	$2.95
☐	23305	THE CONCUBINE	$3.50
☐	20901	SHOES OF THE FISHERMAN	$3.50
☐	20662	CLOWNS OF GOD	$3.95
☐	14074	PROTEUS	$3.50

Prices and availability subject to change without notice.

"Not since SHOGUN has a western novelist so succeeded in capturing the essence of Asia."
—*The New York Times Book Review*

THE WARLORD

BY MALCOLM BOSSE

Ever so rarely, a novel emerges that propels us from our time and place and sets before us a vanished world, made as vividly real as our own. THE WARLORD is such a novel.

China in 1927 is a world of opportunity, of war, of adventure. Caught up in the storm of events are Phillip Embree, American missionary-turned-soldier; Vera Rogacheva, a beautiful Czarist emigree; Erich Luckner, a German arms dealer; and Kovalik, a Russian Bolshevik determined to bring the Revolution to China.

And standing in the eye of the hurricane is General Tang Shan-Teh, both a firm believer in the ancient Confucian values—and in the need for a truly progressive China. He is a man whose power and vision will forever change the face of an ancient, timeless world.

He is the Warlord.

Don't miss THE WARLORD, on sale May 23, 1984, wherever Bantam Books are sold, or use this handy coupon for ordering:

THRILLERS

Gripping suspense . . . explosive action . . . dynamic characters . . . International settings . . . these are the elements that make for great thrillers. And Bantam has the best writers of thrillers today—Robert Ludlum, Frederick Forsyth, Jack Higgins, Clive Cussler—with books guaranteed to keep you riveted to your seat.

Clive Cussler:

☐	22866	PACIFIC VORTEX	$3.95
☐	14641	ICEBERG	$3.95
☐	23328	MEDITERRANEAN CAPER	$3.95
☐	22889	RAISE THE TITANIC!	$3.95
☐	23092	VIXEN 03	$3.95
☐	20663	NIGHT PROBE!	$3.95

Frederick Forsyth:

☐	23105	NO COMEBACKS	$3.95
☐	23535	DAY OF THE JACKAL	$3.95
☐	23159	THE DEVIL'S ALTERNATIVE	$3.95
☐	23272	DOGS OF WAR	$3.95
☐	23737	THE ODESSA FILE	$3.95

Jack Higgins:

☐	23346	DAY OF JUDGMENT	$3.50
☐	23345	THE EAGLE HAS LANDED	$3.95
☐	24264	STORM WARNING	$3.95

Robert Ludlum:

☐	23021	PARSIFAL MOSAIC	$4.50
☐	23232	THE ROAD TO GANDOLFO	$3.95
☐	11427	THE SCARLATTI INHERITANCE	$3.95
☐	22986	OSTERMAN WEEKEND	$3.95
☐	24296	THE BOURNE IDENTITY	$4.50
☐	20879	CHANCELLOR MANUSCRIPT	$3.95
☐	20783	HOLCROFT COVENANT	$3.95
☐	20720	THE MATARESE CIRCLE	$3.95

Prices and availability subject to change without notice.

Buy them at your local bookstore or use this handy coupon for ordering:

SPECIAL
MONEY SAVING
OFFER

Now you can have an up-to-date listing of Bantam's hundreds of titles plus take advantage of our unique and exciting bonus book offer. A special offer which gives you the opportunity to purchase a Bantam book for only 50¢. Here's how!

By ordering any five books at the regular price per order, you can also choose any other single book listed (up to a $4.95 value) for just 50¢. Some restrictions do apply, but for further details why not send for Bantam's listing of titles today!

Just send us your name and address plus 50¢ to defray the postage and handling costs.